Praise for Sean Costello

"Costello knows his way around the mystery/horror genre, and he keeps the action moving and the suspense ratcheted up tight. He is very much a writer to watch out for."
—Margaret Cannon, *The Globe and Mail*

"Sean Costello is a master of the poignancy of everyday living. In *Here After* he tackles a difficult subject with wit and humanity—and a couple of really good scares. It's a father and son story that will touch your heart."
—Susie Moloney, author of *The Dwelling*

"*Eden's Eyes* is the best horror novel I've read since Stephen King's own *Pet Sematary*. A terrific debut."
—*Rave Reviews*

"Sean Costello's *The Cartoonist* is a wonderful blend of horror, psychology, and the power of suggestion that leaves you guessing right up to the very end!"
—*The New Jersey Grapevine*

"Sean Costello is one of the horror genre's brightest new stars and his third novel, *Captain Quad*, will only enhance his position."
—*Other Realms*

Novels by Sean Costello

Supernatural Horror
Eden's Eyes
Captain Quad
The Cartoonist

Thrillers
Finders Keepers
Sandman
Here After
Squall
Last Call

LAST CALL

Sean Costello

Red Tower Publications

Copyright © 2015 by Sean Costello

Cover art Copyright @ 2015 Jelena Gajic

All rights reserved. No part of this publication may be reproduced, distributed or transmitted in any form or by any means, without prior written permission.

Red Tower Publications
Sudbury, Ontario
www.seancostello.net

Publisher's Note: This is a work of fiction. Names, characters, places, and incidents are a product of the author's imagination. Locales and public names are sometimes used for atmospheric purposes. Any resemblance to actual people, living or dead, or to businesses, companies, events, institutions, or locales is completely coincidental.

Last Call / Sean Costello – 1st edition (2015)

Print ISBN: 978-0-9731469-7-4
eBook ISBN: 978-0-9731469-6-7

Author's Note

In a nutshell, *Last Call* is an exploration of the skewed world of the serial killer and the impact their deviant impulses have on the lives of ordinary people.

FAIR WARNING: This one's *not* for the faint of heart.

The inspiration for the novel stems from an admission interview I conducted as a med student on a paranoid schizophrenic who'd just murdered three people. Within the framework of the man's disease—and his otherwise remarkable ability to function and reason in the everyday world—what he'd done seemed to him perfectly justified, no more shocking or deranged than swatting a pesky mosquito. That people like him live and operate among us sparked a grim fascination in me; and with *Last Call*, I've finally gotten around to confronting it in a fictional setting.

Sean Costello

Dedication

This book is dedicated to my good friend and business partner, Mark Leslie Lefebvre. Without his patient encouragement and belief in the work, I'd be watching sitcoms instead of plinking away at the keys, trying to get these stories told. Thanks, Mark.

With special thanks to Ric de Meulles for his unerring critical insights.

PRESENT DAY

1

Saturday, June 27

SUMMER RAIN SWEPT through the alley in ragged, wind-driven columns, choking the storm drains and swamping the uneven pavement. At the dead end of the alley in an alcove of deep shadow, a Maytag dishwasher crate lay on its side, its open end protected from the downpour by a sheet of plastic secured by bricks. Inside the crate huddled a man in his forties, his only possessions the clothes on his back and the twenty-eight cents in panhandled change in his pocket. His skin beneath caked-on layers of grime was jaundiced, and his once clear eyes were rheumy and dull. His limbs bore the telltale pocks of needle tracks, and his scant urine was the color of bong water. People on the street called him CD.

When the rain started the night before, CD had been roaming his usual downtown haunts, stumbling and cursing in a drunken stupor, dully aware that the bottle of Lysol he'd boosted from the Drug-Mart was almost empty, but otherwise oblivious. When the cloudburst drenched him and he began to feel cold, he'd been standing at the mouth of this alley and had spotted the crate. He'd been hunkered inside ever since, sleepless and shivering.

Sometimes in the dark of the crate CD had visions that might have been memories. In these visions he was a rock star, and like he always told the bums he drank with, someday soon he was gonna get the band back together and cut a new album, only these days it wasn't albums anymore it was cds. They told him he was full of shit, but he *knew* he was a rock star because of the tattoo on his chest. It was just a matter of getting back with the boys.

And Sally. Yeah, sweet Sal.

Rain drummed steadily on the roof of the enclosure, saturating the thick cardboard, and CD turned his yellow eyes up in time to see the bellied ceiling burst and a pocket of rainwater gush in to soak him to the bone. Cursing, he rolled onto his hands and knees, tenting the sheet of plastic with his shaggy head. For an instant the world careened and he thought he might black out...but he sucked in a lungful of damp air and held it until the feeling passed. Then he cuffed the plastic aside and got to his feet in the rain.

For a length of time that seemed infinite, CD had been capable of only two sensations: hunger and pain. The hunger was always on him, vast and unappeasable, but only when fed it could he numb the pain. And the pain was awakening fast.

He fished the bottle of Lysol out of his jacket pocket, drained off the last few ounces and tossed the empty aside. Then he headed for the street, singing in a rich, whiskey-hardened voice.

"*Faces come out of the rain, when you're strange, no one remembers your name, when you're...strange...*"

As he shuffled along, working the kinks out, he squinted through the rain to the street, fifty yards ahead. A Toronto Transit bus hissed past followed by a UPS van, and CD reckoned it'd be at least an hour before the liquor stores opened.

He fingered the change in his pocket and knew he had work to do.

That was when he spotted the lone figure at the mouth of the alley. The guy was leaning against the wall out there, smoking a cigarette, and even CD found this odd: standing in the rain with his face upturned like a man basking in August sunshine—and smoking.

CD licked his lips and weaved toward the street, rehearsing his standard spare-changing rap; but when he got within a few feet of the guy, seeing that hard profile now, as bereft of warmth as the sunless sky, some withered instinct urged him to keep walking, head downtown and find an easier mark.

But hunger trumped reason.

"Hey, bro," CD said, unfazed when the man ignored him. The dude was bald, his shiny pate beaded with rain. CD said, "Me and my boys, we got this righteous band— Bad 'n Rude, ever heard of us? We opened for Aerosmith once at the Garden—and we're gonna cut us a cd, soon as we can raise the green. *Not bald*, CD thought, that instinct twitching again. *That big head is shaved.* "So what do you say? Throw in a couple bucks, get your name in the credits?"

"Piss off."

Do what the man says. "It don't have to be dollars. Change'll do—"

The guy turned to face him now and CD saw that he was barely out of his teens, all thick muscle and sneering teeth.

Grinning, the guy said, "You want change?" and CD told his legs to *go*, but then the guy's arm pistoned out and fire erupted in CD's chest, and now the guy was advancing on him, a glint of steel in his outstretched hand.

"I'll give you change."

CD broke into a shambling run, forced back into the alley. It was hard to breathe now, and the warmth on his chest where the guy had struck him was tacky and wet.

"Dead end, ratman. Come get your change."

In his panic CD lost his footing on the greasy pavement and plowed into a drift of trash bags. Hunched over, he could hear the wet suck of air in his chest and realized he'd been stabbed. Breathing was like inhaling shredded tin.

"Wait," he said, getting his feet under him again. "Wait…"

There was a steel service door at the end of the alley and CD threw himself against it, pounding on it with his fists, the effort wrenching something deep in his chest. "Help," he said, the word sounding as if it had been spoken underwater. "Please, open the—"

A powerful hand spun him around and the knife flickered into his belly. CD doubled over and an iron forearm thrust him upright. The man pressed himself against CD with deviant intimacy.

"I'll change you, dipshit."

The knife twisted and rose up and CD's feet left the ground. He had a shining moment of clarity then, and he remembered that he'd once been a boy and that life had been different then.

Blackness spiraled in like soot raised by giant rotors, and before he was lost in it CD had a thought which, even in his extremity, surprised him.

Please, no...I have a daughter...

* * *

Sally West said, "Honey, it's a turd. It's too much money."

Trish West crossed her arms. "Mom, this is the sixth car we've looked at. It's the cleanest and the newest and it's the one I want."

Sally glanced at the tract house into which the owner of this rent-a-wreck had just vanished—"to let you folks hash this out in private"—and spoke in an urgent whisper. "For Christ sake, Trisha, keep your voice down. We can't let this jerk think we're interested." She opened her mouth to recite the several sound reasons she could think of to pass on this overpriced junker, then closed it with a sigh. She felt helpless, an unaccustomed sensation she didn't much care for...and one she'd come to associate more and more of late with her daughter.

Well, Sally thought, *I brought her up to be independent. Too late to change that now.* She said, "Alright, you win. You're twenty years old and what the hell, it's your money. I'll get you some jumper cables for your birthday."

"You mean I can get it?"

Sally said, "You can get it."

Trish smiled and gave her mom a hug, then ran up the path to the owner's front door. The old fox had clearly been observing their deliberations from some unseen vantage, because he appeared at the door an eyeblink ahead of Trish, the pink slip in his liver-spotted hand. The fish was on the hook; it was a simple matter now of reeling her in.

Sally turned her back on the house and this sad little transaction. She hated this part of Sudbury, Nickel Heights. She'd grown up around here and had spent her high school years afraid to walk alone through the streets. She also hated sly, calculating men, like the scuzzy old fart currently hustling her daughter, despised the way they assumed that because you were a woman you'd swallow whole whatever horseshit they handed you, as long as it was served on a silver platter. She'd met too many of them in her twenty years as a single mom.

She leaned against the bucket of bolts that was about to become her daughter's 'new' car—a shit-brown rust-pocked '05 Volkswagen Jetta—and waited, swatting at a mosquito trying to dine on her ear.

***

Ting Chow was chopping vegetables in the kitchen of his father's restaurant when he heard the commotion at the service door. His father often warned him about keeping that door locked, but he was fifteen, curious and imaginative—and his father was in China for the week. Besides, it had been a hell of a racket, sounding to Ting as if some enormous winged creature had flown beak first into the door. It was worth a peek.

He wiped his hands on his apron and unbolted the door, being careful to leave the chain-lock in place. Through the gap he heard a man curse, then flee down the alley. He tried to catch a glimpse of the guy but couldn't get the angle right. A ripple of fear made him slam the door shut and replace the bolt; but not before he heard a moan that sounded more animal than human. And even at fifteen, Ting could identify the cause of that sound: someone was in mortal agony outside his back door.

He grabbed the phone and dialed 911. After giving the address to the dispatcher, he ran into the restaurant to fetch his older brother.

* * *

After Trish handed over the cash for the Jetta—eighteen hundred dollars' worth—and the old man gave her the keys, her mother drove her downtown to the Ministry of Transport, where Trish had to take a number and sit on her behind until some bored clerk got around to serving her; but in spite of her impatience, when her turn came around she put on her most solicitous smile and handed the clerk the required information, along with a bogus receipt in the amount of nine hundred dollars she'd managed to wangle out of the old man. And when the clerk returned her smile along with the receipt, Trish smiled even wider and handed it back, saying, "Don't you need this? To figure out the sales tax?"

"No," the clerk said. "It's all based on book value now."

And that was how Trish ended up paying twice as much tax as she'd anticipated, and the true, ongoing misery of car ownership began to dawn on her.

But she got her official ownership, and her new plates, and left the ministry feeling like a grown-up. A totally broke grown-up. Her mother drove her back to the old man's place, which now looked abandoned, and helped her attach the plates. There was a bad moment when Trish turned the key and was rewarded with only a high-pitched *whiz!*...but after a few more tries the engine caught, belching black smoke, and Trish giggled with delight.

She backed the car out of the driveway and pulled up next to her mother at the curb. As she shifted into Park, the car emitted a thunderous backfire and both of them flinched as if shot. Then Trish rolled down her window and smiled. "Thanks, Mom," she said. "For everything."

Her mother only shook her head.

* * *

Last Call

Sally stood by the idling Jetta, watching her daughter secure her seatbelt—and in that moment such a frightened, sinking feeling came over her that she could barely disguise it. Wrapped up in that feeling was perhaps her first true comprehension of the fact that her little girl was a young woman now, and that she, Sally, was getting older. The fear came at her in a dozen different guises, but ascendant over all of them was the fear of loss. This car symbolized her inevitable loss of control, the abrupt cessation of her ability to shield her child from the world any longer.

Trying to shake it off, Sally said, "So where are you headed, little Miss?" and managed a brittle smile.

"Stacey's place right now," Trish said. "Then, who knows? L.A., maybe. East Texas."

Laughing, Sally said, "Wise ass," and thought, *Don't say it*. But she did. "Be careful, sweetheart, okay?"

"Don't worry, Mom, I will. You taught me how to drive, remember?"

Laughing, Sally said, "That's exactly what I'm worried about," and her anxiety abated just a little. She said, "Okay, kiddo, I gotta run. I'm already late for work. I'll see you and Stacey there at four o'clock sharp. Don't forget."

"I won't."

As she headed for her car, Sally heard her daughter say, "Hey, Mom. Can I borrow some money for gas?" and thought, *And so it begins*.

* * *

Dean Elkind heard the approaching siren and took a deep breath, feeding oxygen to an upwelling of adrenalin. It was only his third week working here in the ER at the Toronto General Hospital and already he was being called upon to perform tasks well beyond his simple portering duties. It was the main reason he accepted all the extra shifts they threw his way and strove to make himself both visible and useful in the department. He knew that if he could prove himself here, when it came time to apply to the emergency medicine residency program—still five years away, but it never hurt to plan ahead—he'd be able to collect some solid letters of reference.

He parked the supply cart he'd been pushing and joined the trauma team in the receiving area. When the stretcher rolled in through the automatic doors, he fell in behind the team as they took over from the paramedics, catching a glimpse of the victim now: male, long-haired vagrant, filthy and unshaven, grimy hand-me-downs, knotted lengths of twine serving as laces for the trashed-looking boots on his feet.

Dean craned his neck for a closer look, seeing the blood-soaked pressure dressings on the man's abdomen and chest. Another of his jobs involved wheeling fatals to the morgue, and he didn't believe he'd ever seen anyone so pale who wasn't already dead. *Poor bastard.* That was one of the scary things about living in a city the size of Toronto, the crazies that roamed the streets unobstructed, the random violence they inflicted only to walk away unscathed.

The trauma suite doors opened and Dean slipped in ahead of the stretcher, positioning himself at the foot of the examining table.

"Okay, Dean," Dr. Isaac, the team leader said, "grab his feet. On three…one, two, *three*."

Then the patient was on the table and a blood pressure cuff was applied, chest leads attached, the tube in his throat hooked up to a mechanical ventilator and the IV bags hung and opened wide.

Leaning over the man now, Dr. Isaac said, "Alright, he's got a pulse. Let's get some O-neg up here and prep arterial and central line trays." He nodded at Dean. "Get these rags off him, chum. He's going to need a chest tube."

Dean went to work on the patient's clothing, hacking through the rain- and blood-soaked fabric with a pair of heavy-duty scissors. He was tugging off the last layer, a moth-eaten Jim Morrison T-shirt, when he noticed the elaborate tattoo on the man's bony chest.

Dean stopped breathing, his adrenalin buzz turning sour.

"Oh, shit," he said. "I think I know this guy."

* * *

Trish pulled the Jetta into the lockstone driveway at Stacey's house and hit the brakes, eliciting a high-pitched screech that triggered a volley of barks from the neighborhood dogs. She rolled down her side window and leaned on the horn, be-bopping in her seat to "Move Like

Jagger" on the tinny car radio. She and Stacey had been best friends since grade school, and Trish was eager to show off her new wheels.

A moment later Stacey came down the steps of her parents' white Colonial, gray eyes fixed on her iPhone, pink ear buds in her ears. Stacey was nineteen, fair-skinned and athletic, with the most amazing head of naturally red hair Trish had ever seen. The girl was decked out in her usual summer attire: faded jean cutoffs, blood red halter top, amber *No Fear* shades and a Toronto Blue Jays ballcap. She stopped partway across the manicured lawn, popped out the ear buds and squealed, "You *got* it."

Trish shrugged like it was no big deal, then let out a squeal of her own.

Stacey scooted around to the passenger side and jumped in, saying, "Cool." Now she bounced on the seat and wrinkled her nose. "Oh, yuk. Smells like bean farts and butt sweat."

Trish turned down the music and laughed. "You should see the fossil we bought it from. But hey, it gets you where you're going, right?"

"Speaking of which," Stacey said, eyes on her phone again, thumbs busily texting, "can we cruise past Randy's place? Please, please, pleeeeease?"

"Girl, you are a glutton for punishment."

"Is that a 'yes'?"

"Affirmative," Trish said. "Just wanna swing by my place first and check the mail."

"Still haven't heard from vet school?"

Trish shook her head and smiled, but she was concerned. It didn't make any sense. All through high school and undergrad she'd been at the top of her class, and the other two kids she knew of who'd applied to Guelph had already got their replies.

Stacey said, "Well, don't sweat it, babe. I sent them some Polaroids from that pajama party we had in the sixth grade. Remember? You? Topless? You're a shoe-in."

Laughing, Trish backed the Jetta into the street.

* * *

Dean checked his watch, then dialed her number again.

* * *

Trish steered the Jetta into the driveway of the small brick bungalow she shared with her mom and stopped beside the porch. She said, "Cover your ears," and shifted into Park. Stacey said, "Why?" and the car backfired, a crisp pistol shot ripping through the tranquil neighborhood. Stacey shrieked and dropped her phone. Trish said, "That's why," and switched off the ignition. The engine ran on for a few beats, then chuffed and quit. "Wanna come inside?"

"Sure. Race ya."

The girls bailed out and tore up the steps, Trish reaching the stoop one long stride ahead of her friend. She unlocked the door and Stacey followed her inside.

The house was full of cool shadow and smelled of sandalwood. *Mom,* Trish thought, *you old hippie chick.* She scooped the mail off the vestibule floor and the house phone rang. As she moved into the family room to answer it, she plucked a plain white envelope out of a stack of junk mail and waved it at Stacey, who smiled and crossed her fingers.

Trish picked up the receiver and said hello. In the brief silence that followed she opened the envelope.

"Trish," a familiar voice said, and Trish's smile collapsed. "It's Dean."

She set the envelope on the phone table, a bitter wash of anger rising in her throat. Anger at herself. She'd believed she'd put this all behind her six months ago…and yet here she was, flushed and trembling at the sound of his voice. *Damn it.* She hated feeling this way.

She said, "I know who it is. I asked you not to call me anymore."

Dean said, "I know, Trish, and I respect that. But this is important."

Stacey came into the room now and picked up the envelope, keeping her eyes on Trish.

"Look, Dean," Trish said, "there's no way I'm going through all this with you again. There's nothing more to talk about."

Stacey said, "Is that Dean? I can't *believe* that dick. Tell him to go hump a goat. Come on, Trish, just hang up. Let's see what the college has to say."

"This isn't about us," Dean said. "It's…about your dad. I think he's here, at the hospital."

Last Call

Trish's knees buckled and she stumbled into the phone table, almost toppling it. One of her mother's figurines wobbled off and shattered at her feet; Trish gazed at it numbly, thinking, *It's about your dad.* She'd waited her whole life to hear someone say those words.

Dean's voice: "Trish? Are you alright?"

She said, "How...?"

"The tattoo. Remember? You told me about it that night."

I remember. "You saw the tattoo?"

"Yeah, and it's just like on the album you showed me. The snake swallowing its tail. Break on Through. Bad 'n Rude. It's all there, right on his chest."

Excitement began to eclipse Trish's shock. "Oh my God. Are you sure? Where did you see him? Is he still there?"

She heard Dean inhaling now, felt his tension through the phone, and her excitement withered into wariness.

He said, "Trish, he's been stabbed."

Trish took a ragged breath. She'd never met her dad. The only evidence she had that he even existed was a rock album he and her mom had recorded before she was born, and a dog-eared photograph of the band, both of which she'd discovered last fall in a trunk in the attic, dusty treasures her mother had somehow overlooked in her stubborn campaign to eradicate all traces of the man's involvement in her life. For years before that discovery Trish had tried repeatedly to find out about him from her mom, but the only response she ever got was, "You don't have a father." Until the night of her fourteenth birthday, when her mother finally relented, tossing her a few bitter crumbs: "He's a bum, Trisha. A selfish, junkie bum. And I hate to have to say this to you, but you're better off without him. We both are." Her mother's eyes had softened then, just a little... "He was an incredible musician, though, I will give him that. He could have been one of the greats." Glad to have her talking, Trish said, "Can you at least tell me his name?" and her mom said, "Mud," and lit the candles on the cake.

Now Trish said, "How bad is it?"

"It's pretty bad," Dean said. "They're taking him to the OR right now. Doctor Peale's working on him, though, and she's the best trauma surgeon in the city." He said, "Look, why don't we give it a couple of hours. I'll see if I can find out how he's doing and call you back. I tried your cell before, but..."

"The battery's charging."

"Will you be at home, then? So I can call you?"

"You're sure about the tattoo?"

"Positive."

"Then I'm coming down. Toronto General, right?"

"Yes, TGH. You want me to meet you?"

"No, Dean, thanks. Thanks so much for letting me know."

"Trish, there's something else. He's been living on the street—"

"No," Trish said. "Please. I want to make up my own mind about him. Goodbye, Dean, and thanks again." She cradled the receiver and turned to Stacey with tears in her eyes. "It's my dad," she said. "I think he's found my dad."

"I heard," Stacey said, embracing her friend. "Is he going to be alright?"

"Dean said it doesn't look good. They're going to operate on him now."

"You weren't serious about going down there, though...were you?"

Trish pulled free of her friend's embrace and headed for the front door, her mind made up.

Stacey went after her, saying, "Come on, Trish, take a minute to think this through. You've never even met the man, that's number one. And what if Dean's wrong? You're going to drive all the way to Toronto on the word of *that* cheating asshole?"

Trish was rooting around in the hall closet now, looking for a jacket, Stacey's words failing to sway her. Couldn't she understand that choice wasn't a factor here? She *had* to go, even if Dean was wrong. She had to know for sure.

Stacey said, "Look, we start our new jobs at four—the jobs your mother had to beg to get for us, remember? She'll crucify you if you don't show up."

"I've waited my entire life for this day, Stace. You know how I feel. I *have* to go."

"Yeah, I get that, but what about...? Oh, screw it, then. I'm coming with you. It's a four hour trip and you're in no shape to drive."

"No. You go to work. No sense both of us losing our jobs. I'll be fine, really. Tell Mom...tell her Dean and I made up. I don't care." She took Stacey's hand. "But whatever you do, don't tell her about my father. Please. I mean it."

"Okay, I promise. But what if it really *is* your dad? You'll have to tell her some day."

"I will, just not today. Wait here a sec, okay?"

Before Stacey could reply, Trish ran upstairs to her bedroom and stuck her cell phone, the band photo and a change of clothes in a knapsack. Then she was back in the vestibule with Stacey, opening the front door, saying, "Come on. I'll drop you off on the way."

* * *

An hour south of Sudbury on Highway 69, Trish swerved into the passing lane and gunned it, leaving a slow-moving convoy of motor homes in her rearview. A few moments later, a trucker in the oncoming lane blinked his headlights at her and Trish checked the speedometer—she was doing a hundred and forty kilometers an hour, fifty over the limit. She eased up on the gas pedal, realizing she'd had it glued to the mat. As she rounded the next bend, doing ninety now, she saw the nose of an O.P.P. cruiser poking out of a tree-lined side road. Cursing softly, she stared straight ahead and drove past, fists clamped to the wheel at ten and two, heart pounding. If he'd clocked her earlier he'd probably impound the car, and if that happened her father might die before she even got to him. The wholly insane notion of trying to outrun the cop entered her mind—Toronto was still three hours away—but repeated checks in her rearview revealed no pursuit.

Signaling now, Trish pulled into a vacant rest stop and shut off the engine. She was wired way too tight. Her hands were cramped from gripping the steering wheel and the long muscles in her back felt like steel cables. She had to calm down. If the man Dean had found really was her dad—and some unshakeable instinct insisted that he was—she'd be no good to him wrapped around a power pole or cooling her heels in a jail cell on a reckless driving charge. Her volleyball coach always told her that the wisest action proceeded from clear, unhurried thought, and she made an effort now to heed that advice. She'd torn out of the house with an empty stomach, twenty dollars in her pocket and nothing on her mind but getting to Toronto as quickly as she could. She had no plan—and worse, hadn't called her mother or left her a note—and no idea of how she'd even approach her father…if he survived his injuries.

She opened her knapsack and took out the band photo, a faded black & white taken in a bar somewhere. In it a young Sally West posed in front of a microphone in skin-tight jeans, stage light flaring through a frizzy afro; and next to her, a shirtless Jim Gamble, vintage hollow-body slung mean and low, the tattoo on his chest glistening with sweat against the pale of his skin. Trish had memorized every detail of his appearance, from the thick tumble of jet black hair and the unmistakable brightness of his smile—no question she'd inherited that trait from her dad — to his cute cleft chin and the lit cigarette tucked ember-up between the tuning keys of his guitar.

Before finding this photograph — and learning that her parents had been recording artists — she'd had only her imagination, and as a little girl she'd retreated to it often: watching her school friends rush into their fathers' arms at day's end and picturing herself doing the same; or sitting alone at her bedroom window, spying on the twins next door playing with their dad on the swing-n-slide and wishing she was one of them.

Growing up, her fantasies had become more sophisticated, and Trish had often envisioned him appearing at her front door at the close of some lengthy and crucial endeavor — working undercover for the police, maybe, or fresh from some decades-long archeological expedition — full of sorrow for his prolonged absence from her life. Discovering he'd been a rock star had only enriched her fantasies.

Sitting here now in the summer heat, Trish remembered the day she'd found the album — and her mother's less than pleasant reaction to the discovery...

* * *

Smiling, excited, Trish came down from the attic with the album in her hand, saying, "Mom, you never told me you and dad were recording artists."

Not smiling, Sally said, "Where did you get that?" and snatched it away from her.

"In an old steamer trunk upstairs."

"Who said you could go through my things? Haven't I told you a thousand times you need to respect my privacy?"

"Yes, Mom, and I'm sorry. I just...I saw that trunk up there and I got curious, that's all. There were some of your old clothes in it and I was trying them on."

Sally aimed an accusatory finger at her, gathering steam for a fresh outburst...and then she laughed. "You tried on those clothes?"

"Yeah," Trish said, hoping the worst was over. She was always startled by the emotional swings any mention of her father could spark in her mother, and today was no exception. In the interest of self-preservation, she tried to cultivate this apparent reversal. "Some pretty cool stuff in there, too, Mom. I especially liked the super-tight T-shirt with the huge marijuana leaf on the front. And those cutoffs? Did you wear those in public or was your butt a lot higher off the ground in those days?"

Sally gave her a fierce stare, but the anger was gone. "Don't try to con me, young lady. I don't appreciate you rummaging around in my things." She grinned. "But, Jesus, you tried that stuff *on*?"

They shared a good laugh over that, and in the end her mother let her keep the album. The only thing she refused to do was discuss it.

"That was a long time ago, sweetie. Your mother was young and headstrong and more than a little foolish. Your father—Christ, I hate even calling him that. The guy who got me pregnant with you is a non-entity to me. He no longer exists, and hasn't for a very long time. I'm sorry you had to grow up without a dad, but there was no way I was letting that son of a bitch anywhere near you. Can you understand that?"

Trish could not, but she held her tongue.

"Maybe someday, when you're older or I figure out what to do with the hate, I'll tell you all about him and ...that time in my life. Until then, my darling, the books are closed." She handed the album back to Trish. "Take care of that, okay? Your dear old ma was pretty hot in those days—I was two years younger than you—and I like to take it out every once in a while and give it a listen. Gloat a bit." She said, "Did you find anything else in that trunk?"

Fearful of reopening a can of worms, Trish said, "No, Mom, that was it."

* * *

Trish put the band photo on the passenger seat and started the car, deciding the first place she saw, she'd stop and get something to eat.

As she merged into traffic, it occurred to her that she'd have to lie to her mom again, this time about why she was in Toronto when she was supposed to be at work with Stacey at the Radisson Hotel.

She stuck to the speed limit now, trying to imagine what her father would be like.

2

JUST OUTSIDE THE city of Barrie, about an hour's drive north of Toronto, Highway 69 became the 400, a well-maintained four-lane along which motorists ripped at treacherous speeds, lane-hopping and cursing each other, prepping themselves for everyday driving in Toronto. Anyone making the trek from the north immediately recalled why they tolerated the protracted winters, the bug infested summers and the apparent cultural void of their chosen home. Internal clocks were wound much tighter down here. Tolerance levels hovered in the red zone. It was a never ending circus of aggressive motion with the city at its congested hub — and it provided a unique brand of cover for its predators. And that, simply stated, was the deliberate blindness of their prey; because it imagined that if it avoided eye contact it became invisible, never realizing that by keeping its head down it made the hunter invisible, even when he stood in plain sight...

Such were the thoughts of a man who leaned against the railing outside a large fast food and filling station complex that flanked the 400, ninety klicks north of Toronto. He stood in plain sight, nursing a milk shake in the muggy heat of midday. The downpour that had drenched the area overnight had ceased as abruptly as it began, the only signs of its passing a few scattered puddles in the parking lot that surrounded the complex. Travelers streamed through here incessantly, either pulling in for gas before merging back into traffic or staying for cold drinks, burgers and fries. To the man leaning invisibly against the railing, they were like ants. Not the constructive, voracious, brutal ants he'd incinerated with a magnifying glass as a kid. No. These ants were sickly mutations, most of them fat and pale, in constant motion but only rarely under their own steam, filing back and forth and filling their faces. For the most part he found them tedious, the majority not worth a second glance.

But there were a few…

With a hunter's patience, he stood in the sun with his soupy milk shake and waited, keen eyes narrowed to slits, constantly scanning.

Now here was something, coming out of the restaurant into the daylight. How had he missed this little beauty? What he liked to call a 'lithe' one. Showing all that skin, little miss supermodel, the whole world her runway. A smile would have been nice, but judging by the rest of her, he was sure it was a sweet one.

He tracked her as she scooted down the steps, bright eyes glued to a cell phone instead of watching where she was going—or paying attention to who was watching her.

Fish in a barrel.

He removed a heavy black sap from his jacket pocket and followed her into the lot. She was moving through the rows of parked vehicles now, oblivious to his silent approach. They came alongside a transport trailer and he raised the sap—

A carload of teenagers screeched to a halt in the driving lane five feet in front of them and the man deftly pocketed the sap. The driver, a stoned-looking mutt with a scruffy beard, hollered out the window, "Hey, Jess, let the farmboy pass," and the girl spun to face him, startled and clearly repulsed, squeezing herself against the side of the trailer to let him by.

He glided past without missing a beat. As he approached the car, he looked directly at the driver and gave him a grin. The kid's wiseguy expression vanished and he looked away.

That's right, asshole. You'd better look away.

He continued his march through the rows of vehicles, moving with the light-footed agility of a cat. When he got to the end of the lot, he circled back to resume his position at the railing.

The day was still young.

* * *

A faded brown Jetta rolled into the lot, belching blue smoke as it slowed. The driver chose a spot between an aging gray campervan and a forest green Porsche 911. The camper belonged to the man leaning against the railing, his milk shake container empty now. When the driver of the Jetta opened her door to step out, the man rose to his full height and pulled off his sunglasses.

A little girl scampering up the steps saw the man move and froze in her tracks, staring at the man in a kind of mute trance. When the girl's father caught up to her, she grabbed his hand and pressed herself against his leg until they were inside the big double doors. Then she ran ahead again.

The man reined himself in now, resuming his position at the railing, becoming invisible again. He knew he should replace the sunglasses, but he wanted to see this one in natural light. As she opened the car door to climb out, a relay flipped in his brain—

And now the clarity was indescribable.

Her tan legs cleared the doorway as she stood, and even from thirty yards away he could see the downy golden hairs on her thighs. Red-painted nails, faded denim cutoffs and a loose green sweatshirt, too hot for this weather and the only disappointment, hiding the athletic torso he knew she must possess. Long neck, blond hair cropped short, eyes sky-blue in a fresh round face.

Crossing the lot now in languid half time, long legs reflected in the puddles. A small boy in a cowboy suit toddled past, running playfully from his dad, and she gave the kid a wistful smile, unleashing a brilliant flash of white that took the man's breath away.

"Glory," he said to no one, slipping his shades back on. "Would you look at that."

It appeared the day had not been wasted after all.

* * *

Last Call

Trish was starving, her bladder full to bursting, and a nidus of pain the size of a chestnut had settled behind her eyes and taken up the beat of her heart. She stepped out of the car into the full force of the afternoon heat and had to steady herself against a wave of vertigo, thinking her blood sugar must be zero. When the feeling passed, she closed the door and started across the lot, noticing the puddles and hoping she wasn't heading into bad weather; it looked stormy off to the east now, thunderheads massing over there against a gunmetal sky.

She smiled at a little cowpoke running from his dad, and was startled when a group of kids came barreling out of nowhere, shrieking and racing past her up the steps. Out of the corner of her eye she saw a creep in a ballcap leaning against the railing, eyeballing her over the rims of his shades, and she looked away, feeling the hackles stir on the back of her neck. She opened the door and went inside.

The restaurant was swarming, the lineups huge, and Trish almost turned on her heel. Then a new cash opened and she was first in line. Five minutes later she was in the bathroom, draining her bladder in a grubby stall and munching French fries out of a take-out bag on her lap.

Five minutes after that, feeling refreshed, she made her way to the exit, wolfing her burger on the fly. Lunch had come to just under five dollars, leaving her with fifteen and change in case she needed gas; although if her fuel gauge was accurate, she still had a little over half a tank left from the fill-up her mother had paid for this morning.

Out on the steps, which were abandoned now, Trish tossed her garbage into a brown receptacle, then hurried back to the car. She could feel the anxiety stirring again, her mind racing ahead into different scenarios ranging from mistaken identity to her father's death to all manner of happy ending. At least the food was stopping her hands from shaking, and she thought the headache might be backing off a little.

She belted herself in and left the swarming lot. As she pulled into the feeder lane and began to accelerate, she passed a gray campervan idling on the shoulder. When it eased into traffic behind her, she failed to notice.

*　*　*

"Shit," Trish said. "Shit, shit, *shit*."

The southbound lanes were grinding to a halt, brake lights coming on ahead of her like falling dominoes. She decelerated and checked her watch.

Two-thirty. Three hours since Dean's call.

God damned traffic.

She brought the Jetta to a stop and it stalled. The dash lights came on and seemed to mock her. She keyed the ignition and produced only a high, breathless *whiz*. The engine didn't even turn over.

"No. Not now. Not today."

Traffic was creeping ahead now, leaving her stranded in the sun. Behind her the driver's door of the campervan

Last Call

opened and a worn cowboy boot clocked down onto the blacktop.

Trish turned the key again and the engine started. She dropped the shifter into Drive and the car lurched forward. Ahead of her, moving at a snail's pace, three lanes merged grudgingly into one.

She inched along with the window open, the backs of her legs tacky against the vinyl upholstery. She was a quarter mile from the bottleneck now, close enough to see that it was road construction causing the holdup—there was a flag girl up there, waving a SLOW sign in the heat shimmer—and not an accident, which was good; it meant there was at least a reasonable chance of getting through without too much further delay. She'd made the trip with her mother once last summer and they'd ended up deadlocked for three hours while cleanup crews first disentangled then towed the wreckage of a seven car pileup. She just needed to be patient.

She was still dating Dean back then, making the journey to his apartment in Toronto whenever she could, usually by bus, depleting her finances and her peace of mind in a vain effort to sustain an increasingly shaky long-distance relationship. She'd met him the previous spring during a week-long stay in Barrie, where she'd been learning to barefoot water ski. Dean was one of the instructors, and Trish was taken by his charm, skill and ambition, not to mention his striking good looks. He seemed so unselfish at first, and Trish fell hard, giving him her virginity a few months later. But he chose to take it in the back of his father's van with a six pack of beer in his belly, ignoring her mild objections about the location and making her feel trampy, just one of many lapses of consideration she began to notice once the fog of infatuation lifted. It wasn't long before the true depth of his self-centeredness became apparent, but by then Trish was committed, determined to make the relationship work…and avoid ending up like her mother, always chasing love away.

A monstrous yellow machine came roaring along the breakdown lane to her left, billowing dust and diesel exhaust. It's towering flank came within a foot of Trish's elbow on the sill, startling her, and she cranked the window shut against the gagging reek of the thing. Within seconds the interior of the car was an oven.

And traffic came to a halt again.

* * *

On a radio signal from Rob Toland, the construction site foreman, Patty Holzer rotated her traffic sign from SLOW to STOP. Rob was approaching her now, all tan and buff and gorgeous coming out of the office trailer, and Patty smiled and thought how appealing she must look in her hardhat, grimy jeans and orange reflective vest.

But when he returned her smile, she knew she had him.

Standing next to her now, Rob pointed north and Patty saw a big CAT 657E scraper lumbering toward them in the breakdown lane. He said, "I need you to make room up here, Patty, help Fletch get that scraper turned around."

"Sure thing, boss."

"Park him on the median for a bit," Rob said. "Hector's ready to blast the overhang off that rock cut down there," pointing south now, "then I want you to move some of this traffic through. If Fletch hasn't fallen asleep by then, get him turned around so we can finish clearing this bottleneck."

"Got it."

Grinning now, Rob said, "We still on for Zak's tonight?"

Patty tilted her hardhat back and frowned. "I thought you made it a policy never to fraternize with the hired help."

"But, I thought we…"

Patty laughed, pleased at how dejected he looked. She said, "I'll *be* there, mister. With bells on. But in the meantime, see if you can't grow a sense of humor."

Red-faced, Rob shook his head and returned to the action. Patty watched him go, admiring the snappy fit of his jeans, then turned her attention to the scraper.

* * *

Aided by the flag girl, the big machine butted in at the head of the line, then angled onto the grassy median. A strident siren blared in the near distance, followed by a thunderous *!whumph!* Trish felt in her feet. Then the flag girl spun her sign and the line was moving again.

Clutching the steering wheel, Trish said, "Come on, come on…" willing the Jetta through the bolthole. She was ten car-lengths from the flag girl now and still moving, the dump truck in front of her creeping along. "Come on..."

She opened the window and an errant breeze blew the band photo off the passenger seat. Trish leaned into the footwell to retrieve it—and when she straightened, the dump truck's rear end was right in her face.

She stabbed the brake pedal and the Jetta stalled. The line ahead began to move. Trish cursed and bit back tears. A horn sounded behind her, then another.

She turned the key.

Whiz!

All the vehicles ahead of her had made it through the funnel, and now twin rows of cement road dividers flanked the Jetta, making it impossible for the other drivers to go around her.

The flag girl was waving her through. A trickle of sweat stung Trish's eye. The yellow machine was backing into the lane up ahead and now the flag girl was shrugging, rotating her sign from SLOW to STOP.

Trish said, "Come *on*, you son of a *bitch*," cranked the key—and the Jetta started. She slammed the shifter into Drive and gunned the engine. The car lunged, spitting gravel, and the flag girl shouted something Trish couldn't hear.

As she shot past the flag girl, Trish saw the yellow machine closing the gap in front of her and every instinct screamed at her to hit the brakes—but she punched the accelerator and deftly squeaked past. When she checked the rearview there was nothing in it but the machine.

"Eat *that*," she said and wound her way quickly through the construction site. When she hit open blacktop again she pushed the Jetta up to one twenty-five, praying she had enough gas left to take her the rest of the way.

* * *

Patty Holzer couldn't believe her eyes. First the ditz in the Jetta, now this asshole in the campervan. When the Jetta took off, he'd booted it too, ignoring her stop sign and coming within an ace of slamming into the side of the scraper. They weren't paying her enough to deal with shitweeds like these.

Maybe it was the heat, but she'd had enough. She marched over to van, ready to tear the guy a new one. He opened his window and she brandished her sign at him, saying, "Can't you read?"

The guy said, "Well, aren't you the frosty cunt," and Patty's anger crumbled into ash. He was grinning at her now, exposing the most grotesque-looking dental work she'd ever seen, perfect white teeth randomly interspersed with decaying stumps. *Like a half-rotten cob of peaches 'n' cream,* Patty thought, shuddering in spite of the heat. His eyes, an odd amber color, sparkled in the sunlight, and his gaze seemed to slither on her flesh. His ears were set low on his head and weirdly malformed, the lobes fused to the angles of his jaw, and he was fondling the ornaments on a snug necklace—small, intricate carvings that looked like ivory—the act somehow deviant, making her skin crawl.

Cutting her gaze away, Patty said, "Please back it up, sir, and wait for the sign," then she returned to her post.

He did not back up.

Patty unclipped her walkie and considered having five or six crewmen come over here to reason with the guy...then she thought better of it. Instead, she called her partner a half mile ahead.

"Clear a path, Sandy. I got a perv up here and I wanna move him through."

"Gonna be about five," Sandy sent back. "Want me to dispatch some of the boys?"

"Negative. Just hustle, okay?"

"Copy that."

Reflecting off the tinted windows, the sun turned the cab of the camper into a black hole, but Patty could feel his eyes on her. "Come on, Sandy," she said in the dusty heat. "Let's get 'em moving."

* * *

The bitch had given him the slip. That made two in one day, which had never happened before, not ever, and he could feel her getting farther away with each furious heartbeat.

This miserable heat. Sweat stung his eyes, stoking his rage. He cranked his side window shut, the heavy tint blocking the sun.

Last Call

There was a time not long ago when his rage had ruled him. At the slightest provocation it sprang up full blown, filling his skull with a tidal roar, and he lashed out at whatever set him off, be it a fridge or a dog or a human being. He was feared, that much was true. But the law got on him. Trouble dogged him all the time. Until he learned how to harness that anger. That rage. He could contain it now, like nuclear energy. When somebody jerked his chain, he could wait, indefinitely if need be, for the reckoning that was bound to come. It was an art he'd learned from a bobcat that hunted his property. He'd spent hours watching and learning. And when he understood, he'd taken the cat's name as his own.

"Bobcat, that's me," he said to the flag girl through the sunblasted windscreen, eyes feasting on her snug, faded jeans. She was on her walkie now, spinning the sign to SLOW, the road ahead clear. She did not look at him.

Bobcat waited. Horns blaring behind him now.

He waited.

Two surly crewmen spotted the situation and strutted up to the campervan, giving him their best badass glares.

And still, he waited.

Until the flag girl looked into the cab. Only then did he inch forward. Though unable to see inside, she gazed directly at him, like a dove in the sway of a cobra.

"Well, girlie," Bobcat said as he rolled past. "Looks like you're the catch of the day."

3

TRISH PULLED INTO the visitors' parking lot at TGH at four o'clock that afternoon. She found a vacant spot near the main entrance and hurried inside, making a beeline for the reception desk. Dean intercepted her before she was halfway there.

"Hey, Trish, I decided to wait."

Startled, flustered, Trish said, "Please, not now." She could feel her face flushing crimson and hated it. *Just leave me alone.*

She resumed her course and Dean said, "Look, I can get you through the red tape a lot faster. Let me do that; then, if you still want me to, I'll go."

Trish nodded and he led her to a bank of elevators. They were alone during the quick ride to the basement and Trish said, "Have you heard anything yet?"

"Not yet. As far as I know he's still in surgery."

The admissions department was across the hall from the elevators and Trish followed Dean inside. One of the girls at a console in there smiled and waved him over. Trish went after him, feeling a pang of something nasty. She buried it quickly, listening as Dean explained the situation to the girl and her manicured fingers worked the keys.

The girl said, "He's listed as a John Doe," speaking to Trish now. "Do you have a name for him?"

"James Gamble."

"Date of birth?"

"December eighth, nineteen seventy-three." She'd found it on the album sleeve, along with the same information on the other band members.

Getting to her feet, the girl said, "Alright. Just give me a minute."

* * *

The bobcat had taught him how to cut his losses. He'd watched the sleek feline stalk a pheasant one day, creeping low through the weeds, closing the distance with infinite patience and stealth; but in the last possible instant as the cat pounced, the bird broke skyward with a startled squawk, leaving only tail feathers in the animal's hungry maw. Unperturbed, the bobcat had slunk back into the trees to content itself with a few tardy field mice and a nice juicy toad, knowing there'd be other pheasants, other days.

And tonight, that was what he, Bobcat, was about to do, content himself with a nice juicy toad.

His gaze was steady, fixed for the past hour on the entrance to a highway roadhouse called Zak's, a rustic watering hole favored by road crews and long haul truckers. The sassy little flag girl had gone in with a guy Bobcat recognized from the construction site—one of the hardons that strutted up on him at the bottleneck, radiating menace—but she'd arrived alone in her own car. With any luck she'd leave alone, too. Not that it mattered.

All he had to do now was sit tight.

* * *

Patty already had a pretty good buzz on when Rob kissed her for the first time. They were out on the dance floor, slow dancing to Patsy Cline's "Crazy" coming out of the jukebox, and Rob leaned in and smacked her one right on the lips. Patty didn't see it coming and their teeth clacked together in the awkward suddenness of it, Rob red-faced now, pulling back, saying, "Oh, shit, Patty, I'm sorry," and Patty put her hands on his face and guided him in for another, this one soft and warm and delicious. And when she said, "You wanna get out of here?" with their lips still touching Rob could only nod his head, the electricity of the moment almost unbearably sweet and exhilarating.

They broke for the exit holding hands, Patty leading the way.

* * *

The roadhouse doors opened and Bobcat's eyes narrowed, his little toad appearing on the arm of the crewman now, both of them looking tipsy. He thought, *Good, makes 'em pliable,* and began to salivate, his pulse rising a few beats. An easy tension surfaced in the muscles of his lean body and his penis stiffened slightly.

"That's it, lovebirds," he crooned in the dark of the camper. He could hear their laughter from his vantage, twenty feet away in the shadow of a bordering maple. He heard her call the guy 'Rob'.

Bobcat thought, *Well, there's gonna be a robbery, alright,* and chuckled at his own wit.

He waited until they reached the rear of the building, then keyed the ignition and followed, switching off the headlights, gravel crunching under the all-terrain tires. He rolled up on them seconds later, hanging on to each other back here, strolling in the moonlight without a care in the world. They didn't even turn around.

Bobcat stopped six feet away from them and flipped a special dash switch, bathing them in the seething light of twin Gobi Stealth LED roof racks. By the time they turned to squint at him, shading their eyes in the glare, Bobcat was striding toward them across the gravel, saying, "That's my little toad you got there."

Rob said, "What the...Patty, you know this guy?"

Bobcat said, "Bitch looks more like a Trixie," and drove the heel of his hand into the guy's nose. The big bastard stumbled but didn't fall, and Bobcat kicked him in the balls with a steel-toed boot, following through with an upcurving elbow that dropped him like a sack of seeds. Finishing with a brutal kick to the ribs, Bobcat leaned over to examine his handiwork and the flag girl swung at him, a ring on her finger grazing his ear, drawing blood. Screeching like a barn owl, she wound up for another shot and Bobcat caught her by the throat, instantly subduing her.

He looked again at Rob, the man unconscious now, and said to Patty, "It appears you'll be needing a new escort," and tapped her with the sap, bearing her up as she sagged into his arms. He carried her to the camper and secured her inside, then got behind the wheel and drove out to the highway, humming tunelessly, confident no one had seen him.

* * *

It was after 6:00 P.M. and still no word from the OR. In spite of Trish's mild objections, Dean had stuck around, bringing her coffee and donuts and sitting with her in the lounge, mostly in silence. He'd left a few minutes ago to check with the OR again, and Trish thought this might be a good time to call her mother…if there was ever going to *be* a good time.

She dialed the number on her cell.

It rang once—

"Do you have any idea the color of shit I had to wade through to *get* you this job in the first place?"

Busted by caller ID.

"I know, Mom, and I'm—"

"No, I don't think you *do* know. I had to do just about everything but sleep with my boss, the sleazy bastard. And you just take off to Toronto?"

"I'm sorry, Mom, you're right. It was impulsive and dumb."

"Oh, it was that and then some. Now you listen to me, young lady. You get your fanny back here by four P.M.

tomorrow—and not a minute later—and maybe, just maybe you'll still have a job." Her tone softened then. "You can't expect to go to veterinary college if you can't afford the tuition."

Smiling, Trish said, "The letter?" and heard paper being shuffled, her mother saying, "And I quote: 'The Ontario Veterinary College, University of Guelph, is pleased to accept your application, and looks forward to your continued academic excellence…'" Which was followed by a wet, unladylike sniff. "You did it, baby. You really did it."

Trish squealed and gave the air a punch, drawing a stare from an old dude tottering past on a walker. She said, "*Yes.* Thanks, Mom. I left in such a hurry I forgot to check. And I'll be home by four, I promise." She saw Dean getting off the elevator, coming toward her now. "I wanna go tell Dean, okay?"

Putting on a catty tone, her mother said, "Stacey told me you two got back together," and Trish could almost hear her grinning; she'd always liked Dean, although Trish had never told her the real reason they'd broken up. "That was awfully sudden. Your dear old ma's gonna wanna hear all *about* this little romantic turnaround."

"*Mom.*"

"Okay, sweetie, go tell him the good news. I'm so proud of you."

"I'm proud of me, too. Bye, Mom."

She signed off and joined Dean at their seats, bright yellow wing chairs by the windows. As she sat Dean said, "They're still working on him up there, but I caught one of the scrub nurses at break and she said he's stable now. Whoever stabbed him got his lung, bowel, spleen and liver, but she said she thinks they'll be done soon."

"That's great news."

Dean said, "So how'd your mom take it?"

Trish could feel herself blushing. "I lied about why I'm here. I hated doing it, but she was already furious at me for taking off." She smiled then. "I got accepted at Guelph."

"Hey, Trish, that's *great* news. I knew you'd make it. I knew it."

Trish could see the sentiment in his eyes, his genuine happiness for her, and an alarm sounded in her heart. She could feel herself being pulled back in and didn't like it.

Dean said, "You know, you haven't changed."

"It's only been six months."

"Seems a lot longer. It's been a weird six months for me. I—"

"Dean, look, I'm sorry, but I've got a lot on my mind right now. God willing, I'm about to see my father for the first time in my life. And like I already told you, I don't want to rake over all that old shit with you again. You made a choice: a crack pipe and Shelley Dixon. Now it's up to you to live with it." She stood. "Maybe you should go. I really appreciate what you've done, but it doesn't change anything between us."

Dean stood now, too, saying, "I understand. I only wanted to say that after you found us, Shelley and me, it really turned me around. I saw a counselor at the university a few days later." He hung his head. "I ended up in a rehab program for twenty-eight days. Had to dump a semester to do it."

He raised his eyes, looking squarely at her now.

"I'm an addict, Trish. I didn't realize it until treatment. I knew something was wrong, but I sure never thought it was that. So I figured, with your dad and all, the way he's been living...maybe I could help."

Trish didn't know what to say.

Dean said, "My life's a lot different now. I have regrets, but I'm learning to live with them. I'm portering here for the summer, then heading back to U. of T. for med school in the fall, and...shit, Trish, I'm sorry. So sorry. And if I can help with your dad, I will. You know where to find me."

He gave her a half smile and started away.

Trish said, "Dean?" and he turned around. She said, "What you did hurt. It really hurt. But what you're doing now, that takes guts. Thanks again for calling me. And if you'd like, once things settle a bit, maybe we can talk. We were friends for a long time; maybe we can at least salvage that."

"That'd be great, Trish, thanks. Want me to wait with you?"

"No, that's okay. I need some time alone."

Dean nodded and walked away.

* * *

Patty Holzer regained consciousness in total darkness. She was cold, lying spread eagle on her back in a moving vehicle—she could feel the vibratory hum of the wheels through the coarse material beneath her—and she believed she was naked, though she couldn't be sure because her wrists and ankles were secured to the floor and she could barely move. She considered screaming for help, but decided against it as her recovering memory filled in the blanks.

Someone had attacked them in the parking lot at Zak's, coming out of the light and beating Rob terribly, then knocking her out and carting her off. And though her head throbbed from the blow she'd taken, her mind was whirring like a computer now, filing back through time to a newscast she'd heard about a month ago: *Another missing girl*, the announcer said. *Gail Grafton, a twenty-three year old college student last seen by her mother as she left their Sturgeon Falls home for a weekend trip to Toronto, where she was scheduled to attend a Shania Twain concert. But Gail never made it to Toronto. Her vehicle was found that evening by police, abandoned in the breakdown lane along a remote stretch of Highway 11, a hundred and twenty kilometers north of Toronto. And though there was no evidence of foul play, investigators are working under the assumption that Gail was abducted; her and four other young women under similar circumstances in the preceding three months...*

Patty began to scream. She screamed until her throat was raw and her struggles against her restraints left her limbs cramped and numb. She screamed until she realized the space she was in was soundproof and that no one was ever going to hear her.

And the tomb that enclosed her rolled on.

After some indeterminate period, Patty felt the vehicle turn and the texture of the surface they were driving on change. Her body was jouncing now, and she heard gravel rattling off the undercarriage like distant machinegun fire.

She closed her eyes and prayed.

And after what seemed like forever, the vehicle stopped. The world went silent for a long beat—then a door swung open and a powerful flashbeam found her eyes, blinding her, and that same cocky voice from the parking lot at Zak's said, "Now I'm gonna loosen this shit off you. You try to kick or take a swat at me, it's gonna go bad for you, understand?" She felt the enclosure shift as he stepped aboard, the light still scorching her eyes. "But I think you're gonna behave for ol' Bobcat, am I right, little toad?"

Sure, you asshole, Patty thought, fear and fury turning her muscles into high-tension cables. She wasn't a small girl, and had been wrestling champion two years running as a senior in high school. *You go ahead and think whatever you want.*

She braced herself as he got closer, ready to kick or bite or gouge his eyes with her fingernails, whatever it took. Then a stinging slap came out of the light and made her eyes water. "Just a taste," he said, sounding amused. "In case you think I'm shitting you. It can go whichever way you want, easy or hard, makes no difference to me."

Keeping the light in her eyes, he sat astride her now and snugged a heavy cloth bag over her head. Then he went to work on the restraints, freeing her right arm first, using a key to release some kind of fixed metal shackle. The significance of that—permanent restraints in a rolling prison—struck Patty with a hundred times the force of the slap he'd given her, and she realized this really *was* the guy who got all those other girls...and not one of them had turned up yet, dead or alive.

A paralyzing horror welled up in her and she bit down hard on her lip to stifle it. *No,* she thought, trembling now, the night air pulling her skin into gooseflesh. *You've got to stay sharp.*

Once he'd freed her feet, he shifted his weight to work on her other hand, bracing a knee across her throat now, making it difficult to breathe.

"Now remember what I said. You treat Bobby right, why, maybe I'll let you go back home to your momma when we're done. You believe me?"

"Yes."

"It speaks." He slapped her again, harder this time. "You'll be good, then?"

"Yes."

"Show me some of the tricks you were gonna do for young *Rob*?"

"I'll do whatever you want. Just, please, don't hurt me."

He rose and jerked her to her feet. "That's so sweet."

He led her to the doorway now—Patty could feel the night air rushing in—and hopped outside, the enclosure shifting as his weight dropped away. When his hand closed around her wrist to pull her through, Patty threw a fierce kick—but all she struck was thin air and now her bracing foot lost its purchase, dropping her onto her backside in the doorway. There and then gone, he'd sidestepped her attack with a quickness that startled her and set that numbing terror loose in her again.

He said, "See? I *knew* you'd be the feisty one," and punched her in the face.

Patty slumped through the doorway into the wet grass.

* * *

Gail Grafton heard the camper pull into the yard and huddled against the wall of the earthen pit under the barn. The base of the pit was flooded with ground water from a recent rain and Gail was freezing, her nude frame showing ribs and knobs of bone from starvation and prolonged exposure. She'd been in the hole almost a month, though any clear sense of time had long since abandoned her, along with the bulk of her sanity. She was pure animal now, any semblance of humanity obscured by pain, constant fear and the absence of any real nutrition. Things crawled into the eight-foot diameter hole from time to time, and Gail had learned to subsist on them. The first thing she'd eaten was a milk snake that had fallen into the pit from the barn up above. That had been on day six, when Gail was still aware enough to keep track of the days by the shifting patterns of light and dark she perceived through the air holes in the thick metal plate that covered the pit. The snake had startled her, slithering across her ankles in the dark, and she'd picked it up by the tail and whipped it against the root-stubbed wall, stunning it. The skin had been scaly and tough, but the meat was quite good, chewy and moist. Little that satisfying had come along since.

She listened with an alertness she'd never known in her previous life as a student living with her mother at the age of twenty-three, a life that had already faded from memory and sunk into this pit of despair. There had been another girl down here when Gail was shoved in naked and bleeding, a girl who had stared at her with terrified eyes, so far gone that all she could do was shake her head and moan like a beaten dog. And on the third night, Gail heard the camper pull into the barn — and then the dark shaft was flooded with light, glaring, retina scorching light, and when it was extinguished Gail was alone in the hole in the ground. A few minutes later she heard the screams, faint with distance, but shrill enough to curdle her blood.

And then the chainsaw, silencing the screams.

So she listened. And waited.

* * *

Trish had begun to drowse when a tiny, bright-eyed woman in faded scrubs sat next to her in the visitors' lounge. "Trish?" the woman said. "I'm Doctor Peale. They tell me you're our John Doe's daughter."

"Yes. I think so. It's complicated. His name is Jim Gamble."

"Well, it looks like he's going to pull through. He's very lucky. But the road ahead will be a rough one. God only knows what he's been poisoning himself with. On the bright side, guys like him are usually tough as nails."

Trish said, "Where is he now?"

"In ICU."

"Can I see him?"

"Of course you can. Come with me."

Trish followed the surgeon through a set of orange doors marked SURGICAL INTENSIVE CARE. When they arrived at cubicle 9, the curtain drawn in there, the doctor said, "I just want to prepare you a bit before you go in. He's on a ventilator right now and he's been heavily sedated, so he won't be aware of you at all, do you understand?"

Trish nodded, feeling the thump of her heart in her throat.

"He looks pretty beat up, I'm afraid," the doctor said, "but he's stable and I'm optimistic." She smiled and placed a warm hand in the small of Trish's back, guiding her toward the cubicle door. She said, "Just come ahead out when you're done," then hurried away, pulled by other duties.

Trish drew the curtain and went inside. The room was dim, the big railed bed centered in the cramped enclosure. A bank of monitors glowed above the head of the bed and a cluster of blood bags hung from an IV pole on the left. Motionless on the bed lay a man who at first glance looked nothing like her father; but several years had passed since that photo was taken and people changed. Still, instinct told her there was no way this shaggy, skull-eyed vagrant could be her dad, and above everything else she felt relieved. Because if this really was her father, she wasn't sure she could handle it. Not this.

No. She'd find her real dad someday, someday soon, and together they'd work things out, build some kind of future together.

Trish moved closer to the bed, studying the man's face more closely now. Gingerly, she lifted one of his eyelids, revealing the same sky-blue color she'd inherited. She let the lid go and raised the blanket off his chest.

And there it was, the same tattoo, exact in every detail.

Trish remembered something else then, a puckered scar she'd noticed on the dome of his right shoulder on the album cover...

It was there.

Trish said, "Dad?" and cried for a while, holding his calloused hand. Then she pulled up a chair and began to wait.

* * *

Patty came to propped upright in an old barber chair that had been fitted with Velcro restraints, the one across her chest so tight she could hardly breathe. He'd taken the bag off her head, but she could still smell the musty fabric. Her bottom lip was split, and blood trickled into her throat from her broken nose, making her want to vomit. Bobcat was nowhere in sight, but she could hear him in a nearby room, clattering through what sounded like kitchen utensils. From what she could see in the poor light, she was in a workshop of some kind, with a wooden workbench and an assortment of tools arrayed on pegboard.

Startling her, a small dog jumped into her lap, a frisky Jack Russell terrier, the mutt licking the blood off her chin now.

Then that metallic clattering ceased and the lights came on.

He was beside her now, but she couldn't see his face. She heard him say, "Oh, you're awake," like she'd been having a pleasant nap. Then to the dog, "Sammy, get down out of there," and the dog jumped to the floor and curled in a wicker basket.

He moved and now Patty could see him, just his back as he stepped past her to place something on the workbench; whatever it was, she caught only a glimpse—ten or twelve inches long, snugly bundled in terrycloth—but when he set it down on the bench, it sounded like whatever he'd been working with in the other room, steel against steel, like knives and forks.

Then he turned and Patty saw his face.

"You," she said and he smiled, showing those teeth.

"None other."

"Who *are* you? What do you want?"

"Fuck, girl," he said with an obscene chuckle, "don't you know shit? I'm what happens when you get in people's way." He stood in front of her now and unzipped his fly. "But to business. How about you suck me off, real nice, then I let you go. How'd that be?"

Patty said, "Okay," no fight left in her.
"You wouldn't tell anybody about this, would you?"
"I won't tell."
"Well, alright."
He had the trace of an accent. *Southern*, Patty thought.

He shuffled closer and Patty swallowed her revulsion and closed her eyes, praying she wouldn't gag. She'd keep her eyes closed and think about getting home and give him the best damn blowjob he ever had...and then maybe, please God, just maybe, he really *would* let her go, drive her blindfolded to the highway and throw her in a ditch, it didn't matter. As long as he let her go. She hadn't really seen anything yet, just a glimpse of a rundown farmhouse in the dark and she would never tell a soul—

"I'm thinking you'd bite ol' Bobcat."

"No, please, I'll do whatever you want."

"You promise?"

Patty nodded, the motion impeded by the restraints. A tear rolled onto her lips and she licked it away.

"Shit, I don't know. You look like a biter to me."

She heard him zip his pants, then retrieve the bundle off the workbench. She opened her eyes.

"I'm betting that smart mouth of yours'd look prettier with no teeth in it anyways."

Bobcat stepped on a pneumatic pedal and the chair-back dropped, the illusion of falling making Patty cry out—then she saw the dental forceps in his hand and screamed.

He pulled an overhead surgical spot into view and switched it on, the glare bringing water to Patty's eyes.

Strangely, he apologized and adjusted the beam to focus on her mouth.

Patty tried jerking her head aside, bucking against the restraints, but she was completely immobilized.

He sat on a stool and leaned over her head. "Now open up."

Patty clamped her jaws shut, and when he forced the instrument into her mouth she bit down on it as hard as she could.

"See? I *knew* you was a biter."

He punched her in the stomach, knocking the wind out of her, and Patty had to gasp for air. "Come on, little toad," he said. "One way or another, this is gonna happen. Might as well open up."

She was helpless now, too weak to fight him anymore, and she felt the cold steel forceps glide into the back of her mouth. She gagged—and then screamed in pain as Bobcat's hand came up with the forceps, a bloody molar in its jaws. He dipped the tooth into a jar of water, swishing it around, then held it up to the light, appraising it.

"Fillings. Useless."

He tossed the tooth onto the floor and Patty saw the Jack Russell scoot over to give it a sniff.

The forceps went in again—grasped, rocked—and came out with another tooth, an incisor this time, and Patty screamed in horror and pain, her clutching fingernails fracturing against the metal arm rests.

Outside, in counterpoint to Patty's cries, dogs began to bark and howl.

After a brisk rinse and a cursory inspection, Bobcat dropped the incisor onto the floor, saying, "Useless." Saying, "*Fuck* me, now you got them damned shithounds stirred up," punching her again.

Patty could feel herself slipping into darkness.

"Wasting my time. Gonna be up fuckin' with you all the damn night. Now *open up.*"

* * *

Trish said, "You don't know how long I've waited for this moment. How many different ways I've imagined it." She glanced around the ICU cubicle and laughed, a clipped, humorless sound. "This certainly wasn't one of them."

She knew he couldn't hear her, but it needed to be said.

"Mom would never tell me about you. Whenever I asked, she'd just say, 'You don't have a father'. So I stopped asking. Then I found some of her things in a steamer trunk. Pictures, old letters, stuff like that. The album you guys made was in there, too. That was unbelievably cool. You and Mom, recording artists. I nearly wore that record out listening to it."

She squeezed his hand. "There was this one photograph; you and the band in a bar someplace. I knew it was you right away. I spent hours just staring at that photo, memorizing every detail of your face. Wondering where you were. How you could have left me. Funny, I never blamed you. I guess I blamed Mom. And myself. I started looking for you after that. Tracked down some of the other band members. But no one knew where you were. One said Toronto, another L.A. Your bass player figured you were dead.

"But I never gave up. We'll work it out. You'll see, Dad. We'll work it out..."

* * *

In the pit under the barn Gail Grafton stopped breathing and froze, her hearing preternaturally keen in this animal state. There was a scream, distant and shrill, like a death cry peeling across a savanna. Then the chainsaw rattled to life and the screaming ceased.

Gail remembered the chainsaw.

She squeezed herself into a crouch against the dirt wall and began to rock, hands clapped over her ears, dry tongue running her raw, toothless gums.

4

Sunday, June 28

JUST AFTER SUNRISE, site foreman Rob Toland parked his Jeep in front of the mobile office trailer and switched off the ignition. It was still early and only a few crewmen had arrived ahead of him, a small circle of them standing by the Porta Potties, smoking cigarettes and drinking coffee.

Before getting out of the vehicle Rob checked himself in the rearview, thinking, *Fucking mess*: nose taped; two black eyes, the left one swollen shut; a goose egg the size of a golf ball in the middle of his forehead. *Jesus.*

He got out of the Jeep, not moving very fast.

Rudy, one of the machine operators, was approaching him now, saying, "Man, you look like shit. What happened? You try some errant moves on that flag girl last night? Jesus, look at you. *Yo, Adrian!*"

Rob touched his nose, then his swollen eye. "Son of a bitch blindsided me. Broke my damn beak. Didn't even see it coming."

"You an ugly motherfucker anyway."

"Fuck you, Rudy. You seen her yet?"

"Who, Patty? Nope."

Rob scanned the site, eager to get some answers. Like why he'd come to at one in the morning in the dirt behind Zak's all by himself. Had she really just *left* him there? And who was that psycho? An ex boyfriend she neglected to tell him about? Or a *hus*band? No matter which way he imagined it, he couldn't get his mind around it.

There was no sign of Patty, but what he did see pissed him off: one of the big CAT 5230 excavators with the bucket left straight up in the air.

He said to Rudy, "Where's Ziggy?"

"Not here yet, boss."

Cursing, Rob headed for the excavator. "How many times do I have to tell that shit stain to lower his bucket when he's done for the day."

Trailing him, Rudy said, "Shit for brains."

Rob climbed aboard the machine and fished through the ring of keys on his belt—then he spotted a tangle of multicolored wires, some of them spliced, hanging out of the ignition panel.

"What the hell?"

He glanced at Rudy ten feet below sipping coffee, then tried the key and the engine started, spewing diesel exhaust as he gunned it. After giving it a minute to warm up, he worked the controls and the bucket began its descent, tilting forward as it came down.

He could see Rudy watching, saw his eyes widen as something slid out of the bucket to land at his feet, Rudy leaning in for a closer look now, saying, "Sonny Jesus," and dropping his coffee in the mud as something else hit the ground, more heavily this time. Rob could hear it over the din of the machine, splashing into the muck as it landed, but couldn't tell what it was.

Now several more objects Rob could see only in glimpses—pale, shapeless chunks—struck the ground and Rudy spun away to puke up his breakfast. Rob left the bucket ten feet up in the air and jumped off the excavator, jarring his ribs where his attacker had kicked him. And when he saw what it was, he felt his own stomach lurch and he looked away, up at the hovering bucket.

He saw Patty Holzer's severed head up there, toothless and so terribly pale, teetering on the edge of the blade, staring down at him between the bucket's blunt teeth.

* * *

Dean said, "You really have to leave so early? I could buy us breakfast. It's cafeteria food, but it's not so bad. You sat in that cubicle all night, Trish; you really should eat something."

He was leaning on the sill, close enough that Trish could kiss him through the open window if she decided to, and it annoyed her vaguely that she was okay with that. She said, "Thanks, Dean, but I really should be going. I had some car trouble on the way down and I can't risk being late for work. Not if I want to live."

"Well, don't worry about your dad, okay? It'll be days before he even knows where he is. I'll keep an eye on him for you, and I'll call you with updates every day."

"That'd be great...but if you happen to call the house and my mom picks up, please, don't say anything to her about this."

"You have my word."

Trish could feel her face flushing again. *Damn it.* She looked at her feet and said, "She thinks you and I made up."

He smiled. "How would you rate the chances of that actually happening?"

But the wounds were still too fresh. "Let's just see how things go, okay?"

Touching her arm, Dean said, "Sounds good to me." He straightened now, stepping away from the car. "Safe trip. I'll call you tonight."

Managing a tired smile, Trish thanked him again for the gas money he'd loaned her and pulled away.

* * *

By 6:30 that morning the construction site had morphed into a full-blown crime scene, a half dozen cruisers parked helter skelter, detectives and technicians milling around, the excavator cordoned off with bright yellow barricade tape.

Near the loader a slim, graying detective named Dan Boland stood in conference with a colleague, Alec Dunster, a fireplug in his late thirties with a twitchy, impatient manner.

Speaking around the cigar in his mouth, Boland said, "Get anything useful out of the date?"

Last Call

"Says he didn't get a good look at the guy," Dunster said. "Sounds like he was seriously shitfaced at the time. All he knows about the girl is she was engaged once. She told him it was old news, but he said the perp said something like 'That's my little toad' before putting his lights out. Some first date."

Boland nodded, saying, "Still, it's worth a follow up. The girl's family should be able to put us in touch with the ex." He was watching Forensics bag the vic's remains. "You get a look at that head?"

"Sick puke yanked all her teeth."

"Doesn't make any sense."

* * *

At 3:46 that afternoon, Trish tore out of the house still buttoning the blouse on her hotel staff uniform. Her hair was a mess, she couldn't find her obligatory name tag, she was supposed to punch in at 4:00 o'clock sharp and the hotel was a sixteen minute drive from her front door, *if* she made all the traffic lights.

She caught her toe running across the lawn, cursed and almost fell. A kid on a trike across the street quit picking his nose to stare at her. It started to rain. She piled into the Jetta and turned the key—

WHIZ!

"*Shit!*"

It was all she could do not to scream. Not only had the excitement of owning her first car already worn off, in this moment—with the clock ticking and sweat running in rivulets between her boobs in this hideous, baby shit-colored blouse—what she really wanted was to take this clunky piece of crap back to its previous owner and torch it on his scabby front lawn.

Her mother had been right.

She checked her watch. Another minute gone. She thought of calling her mom to say she'd be late, but that would be like asking for the death penalty. If she kept her trap shut, she might still be able to sneak into the hotel undetected.

Her fingers itched to turn the key, but she knew from bitter experience that it was best to give it a few minutes.

She sat there watching raindrops spatter the dusty windshield, reflecting on her insane trip home, a four-hour drive costing her six-and-a-half. She closed her eyes and saw Dean leaning on the sill, asking if she really had to leave so early.

The trip had started out fine, her 9:00 A.M. departure sparing her the worst of morning traffic. She made the 400 in record time, and had enough gas left over to carry her all the way up to Highway 69. Whatever else her 'new' car might be, it was really excellent on gas. She stopped north of Barrie to top up the tank—and after she paid the attendant, the damned thing wouldn't start. A guy at the next pump said, "Sounds like your starter's going," And Trish thought, *You think*? She was no mechanic, but the diagnosis seemed fairly self-evident—and it didn't help. She tried cranking it again right away, but the *whiz* turned into something much worse, a kind of breathless death rattle that made her cringe. So she got out in the muggy heat, grabbed a Coke out of the pop machine and paused to take a long swig and stare bullets at the Jetta. And when she got back in the car a few minutes later, it started on the first try.

That had been bad enough, but the real time waster came at the construction site that had held her up the day before. She'd forgotten all about it, and when she got jammed in it again she cursed herself for not keeping it in mind and planning an alternate route. As before, the merge to a single lane took forever, and the truly annoying part was that from a distance it didn't appear as if anyone was actually working over there, the machines all standing idle.

But then she saw the police cruisers and the crime-scene tape, and there was a cop standing next to the flag girl at the choke point now, the officer leaning in to speak to each of the drivers in turn, slowing things down even more. When Trish got four car-lengths away the Jetta stalled, and in her fear of holding things up she tried to start it right away—and this time that wretched death rattle was punctuated by a crisp backfire, the report so loud the cop actually reached for his sidearm.

In a dreadful kind of déjà vu, the vehicles in front of her cleared the check point one by one and now the cop was waving her ahead, impatient in the sweltering heat.

Trish turned the key and the Jetta shrieked. She shrugged at the cop and tried on a smile that didn't fit. The flag girl came to the window and said, "You'd better get it moving, Miss. Fuses are pretty short around here already."

"You want to give it a try?" Trish said and the girl unclipped her walkie and turned away. She said something Trish couldn't hear, and a few moments later three grim-looking crewmen appeared. The flag girl told her to put it in Neutral, and the men pushed the Jetta up to the cop like it was a kid's toy. The cop showed her a picture saying, "Do you recognize this girl?" and Trish did, right away. She said, "Yes, I saw her here yesterday," and pointed to the shoulder of the equally backed-up southbound lanes. "Right over there. She was working, holding a sign."

The cop thanked her and said she could go, and Trish was left to wonder what had happened here. The crew guys pushed her out of the way and she spent the next forty minutes waiting for a gracious on-site mechanic to come have a look under the hood. Thirty minutes after that they got the car started and the mechanic told her it was probably her starter.

Starving by this point, she broke for lunch at a truck stop restaurant and got underway again as quickly as she could. North of Pointe au Baril there was a car accident that cost her an hour, then she got caught in a cloudburst so intense she had to slow to a crawl for the next fifty kilometers.

And now she was late.

She turned the key and the Jetta started.

* * *

Last Call

When Detective Boland entered the police mortuary in Barrie that afternoon he found the pathologist, Dr. Franklin Todd, hunched over a high-powered microscope, numerous glass slides littering the table in front of him. Mozart played softly in the background, Piano Concerto No. 24 in C minor, one of Dan's favorites. The music soothed him.

Without looking up, the pathologist said, "Afternoon, Dan. Just finishing up the microscopic."

Smiling, Dan said, "How'd you know it was me?"

"Those infernal cigars. You reek." He raised his eyes now, flicking the bifocals off his forehead to land neatly on his nose. "I've got some lung cancer slides that might smarten you up. I have my teaching stuff around her somewhere..."

"Never mind," Dan said. "If Connie can't make me quit, what chance do you think you have?"

"Stubborn bastard."

The pleasantries dispensed, Dan said, "So what can you tell me, Frank?"

"For starters, you're dealing with an exceedingly bent piece of work here. This is one sick puppy."

"You're supposed to tell me something I don't already know."

"Your perp did the dental work while the lady was still alive. Chainsawed her alive, too." He indicated the slide on the scope. "I found microemboli in the lungs. Traces of machine oil and bits of sawdust. This can only happen if the heart is still beating."

The doctor swiveled a computer monitor around to face the detective, then clicked on a tiny photograph, the shot enlarging now to fill the screen.

"And here. A one-and-a-half inch incision in the abdominal wall, also inflicted antemortem. Neatly done. Almost surgically precise."

"Any signs of rape?"

"I suppose you could call it that," the pathologist said. He tapped the screen with the tip of his pen, indicating the small incision. "Stated bluntly, Dan, the guy made a hole in her belly and fucked her in the guts."

Dan Boland rubbed his eyes with the heels of his hands. In his nearly twenty years in Major Crimes, he'd witnessed more than his share of the twisted shit people dreamed up to do to each other, but this one ranked in the top five.

"Jesus," he said.

* * *

At 4:00 P.M. on the button, Trish slipped in through the kitchen doors at the Radisson Hotel and fell in next to Stacey, the girl already busy wrapping utensils in burgundy napkins. She saw her mother on the phone in her glass-walled office, staring daggers at her now, and said, "Uh-oh."

Stacey said, "Wouldn't wanna be ya," and Trish elbowed her in the ribs. She cut her eyes away from her mother's death stare, picked up some utensils and got busy.

Sally strolled over a minute later and Trish thought how sharp she looked in her businesswoman's suit, the word SUPERVISOR embroidered in gold on the breast pocket. She said, "Hi, Mom," but her mother kept walking, moving behind her now, leaning over to say in her ear, "That was close, little sister. Very close."

Out of the corner of her eye Trish saw Stacey smirking and had to bite her tongue to stifle a giggle. Her mother slapped her on the fanny and Trish let out a squeal.

Strutting away, her mom said, "Next time wear your name tag," and the girls lost it, their laughter peeling through the stainless steel kitchen.

* * *

An hour after her shift ended, Trish crawled into bed and leaned against the headboard, as exhausted as she'd ever been. Dean had called while she was still at work to tell her nothing had changed. At least her dad was still alive.

She took the band photo off the bedside table and viewed it in the lamplight, thinking, *I finally found you.* She prayed he'd make it through.

She tucked the photo in the night table drawer and switched off the lamp. "Nite, Dad," she said in the dark of her room. "Sweet dreams."

* * *

In his ICU bed at TGH Jim Gamble lay stock still in the dim light, the only sound the steady hiss and chuff of the ventilator that kept him alive.

5

Monday, June 29

JIM GAMBLE OPENED his eyes.

His first perception was pain, his old companion, but on a scale beyond any he'd previously experienced; it was prodigious, apocalyptic, and his body braced against the enormity of it. This intense sensation did not reach his higher centers, however, for these were still beyond function; but on a primitive level, where the animal lived, billions of neurons discharged in tandem in a pyroclastic eruption of agony. It was centered in his belly, where the hunger waited, and the muscles of his core drew him into a bow, causing the jagged suture line to let go.

His gaze settled on the ceiling now, his eyes bulging in horror. The tiles up there were swarming with spiders, goliath black tarantulas, and they were losing their footing and falling, dozens of them landing on his face and chest and legs, skittering hordes of them covering the bed.

He opened his mouth to scream, but the breathing tube rendered him mute. He cranked and twisted his arms until his wrists popped free of their padded restraints, and now his hands came up and yanked the tube from his throat, giving voice to his horror. Screaming, he sat bolt upright in bed, sending a pole laden with med pumps crashing to the floor.

The staff that rushed in to restrain him had eggplant heads and smoldering red eyes and Jim fought them with everything he had, opening his suture line even more. He howled like a lunatic. "Get them *off* me! *Get them off!*"

Then something warm crept up his arm like gentle surf, finding his brain, and Jim Gamble drifted away on it, to a place where nothing mattered.

* * *

Trish was pulling on her uniform when her cell phone rang. It was Dean.

"Hey, Trish."

"Hey, Dean, how—oh, my God, was that a scream?" It had sounded like someone being burned alive.

Dean snickered. "Yeah, I'm in the delivery room. I just brought a teenage girl up from the ER. Poor thing had no idea she was even pregnant. Her grandmother brought her in—these two, they look like something out of *Deliverance*, six teeth between them and no shoes, three hundred pounds each and neither of them over four feet. Granny brought her in with abdominal pain, thinking it was something she 'et'. Turns out she's fully dilated. On the elevator she asked me when the belly button opens up so the baby can come out."

"Oh, my *God*."

"Yeah, never a dull moment. Speaking of which—and I don't want you getting too excited; things are still pretty grim—but your dad's awake."

Trish smiled. Awake was better than comatose. She said, "That's fantastic." And then, "What do you mean 'grim'?"

"He's in the DTs—delirium tremens, acute alcohol withdrawal—and it's not very pretty. Hallucinations, convulsions, irritability. He could still even die."

"That means he's going to need me."

"They had to sedate him pretty heavily, Trish. Maybe you should put off coming down for a while. He doesn't even know where he is yet."

"I'm coming tomorrow after work. It's all arranged. I'll be staying with my aunt in Mississauga."

"I just figured you might not want to see him like this."

"I can handle it, Dean. I'm a lot tougher than you think. I want to be with him when he wakes up again."

"Okay. Maybe I'll see you?"

"Sure. Maybe. Thanks for keeping me posted."

Trish signed off and finished getting dressed, then Googled delirium tremens on her phone. It was just like Dean had said. The next several days would be dicey in the extreme, and in a case like her dad's, where chances were good he'd been ingesting substances much more toxic than booze, death was a real possibility.

She wished she could take off right now, but she had a double shift at the hotel and her mother was right, she needed the money.

She grabbed her knapsack and headed for the car.

* * *

Bobcat parked the camper in front of the Cold River Trading Post and pocketed the keys. The parking lot was packed today, but that was how he liked it. The bigger the crowd, the harder he was to see.

With a glance in the rearview, he snugged the ballcap over his eyes and combed his fingers through his tangled beard. Sammy, his Jack Russell terrier, eyed him expectantly from the carrier in the passenger footwell, but Bobcat said, "Not this time, Sambo. You go on back to sleep now, boy. Bobby'll be right back." He retrieved a small rectangular item wrapped in cloth from the seat beside him and exited the vehicle.

The bell above the shop door startled him, and not for the first time Bobcat wanted to rip the damned thing off its mount and ram it down the throat of the fat fuck proprietor—Hank—the man eyeballing him now from his throne in front of the register. Patrons were scattered all through the sprawling shop, but at the moment Hank was alone at the register.

"Hey, Bob," said the fat fuck, like they were old pals, "what've you got for me today?"

Stretching his face into what passed for a smile, Bobcat said, "Hank, my boy, I got some real beauties for you today." He saw the man staring at his teeth, a grimace on his doughboy face, and slid his lips shut. "Yep, some real beauties."

Last Call

Bobcat stood across from the man at the display counter now and made a show of removing the cloth from a red-felt jewelry box that had belonged to his mother. He centered it on the glass countertop and pried it open, turning it to face Hank.

"Oh, my," Hank said, seating a jeweler's loupe over one eye as he leaned in for a closer look. "You, sir, are an incredible craftsman. The detail in these is spectacular. Better than the last batch if you ask me."

Bobcat thought, *Yeah, well, nobody asked you.*

Hank said, "Are you ever gonna tell me what they're made of?"

"Trade secret, Hank."

"And you're sure it's not ivory."

"That'd be illegal. You want 'em or not?"

Hank let the loupe drop into his palm and straightened, giving Bobcat a wary smile. "Sure I do, Bob. 'Course I do." He pulled out a small gray cashbox and keyed it open. "The usual price?"

Bobcat nodded, pocketed the cash and left without another word. It was a beautiful day in cottage country.

A perfect day for hunting.

* * *

But the day turned out to be a disappointment. Nothing but skanks and fatties at his regular spots, and there seemed to be more than the usual scattering of O.P.P. cruisers buzzing the two-lane today. *Probably looking for me*, Bobcat thought, oddly pleased by the notion. *Like they're ever gonna find me.*

Sammy was on his lap now, and he patted the little guy's head, saying, "Well, Sambo, shall we call it a day? Head back to the ranch and boil up some dogs?" The terrier regarded him with worried eyes, his stubby tail no longer wagging, and Bobcat said, "*Hot* dogs, little buddy. Boar's Head franks, your favorite. I'd never eat you. Hardly enough meat on them bones to make a meal any—"

There was movement up ahead now and Bobcat tensed, Sammy scooting across the bench seat to stand on his hind legs, front paws propped on the dashboard, sharing his master's view.

Accelerating, Bobcat saw two young women standing on the shoulder of the oncoming lane with their thumbs out, heavy-looking backpacks at their feet. They weren't wearing much—tank tops, skin-tight cutoffs, hiking boots—and Bobcat said, "Well, kiss my ass, Sambo, there *is* a god. And ain't he a prick?"

He drove past the girls with his window shut and his gaze aimed straight ahead, paying them no heed. When they were out of sight, he slowed in preparation for a U-turn—and now a souped-up Duster appeared in the oncoming lane, occupied by two teenage boys.

Bobcat said, "Shit," and braked, pulling a U-ie the instant the muscle car passed, saying, "No way, Sammy. No *way* those dinks are gettin' them toads."

Within seconds he was riding the Duster's tail, and now he tramped on the go pedal and passed them at speed, the kid leaning on the horn back there and flipping him the bird.

The girls were just a few yards ahead now, watching with their mouths open, and Bobcat hit the brakes, the Duster roaring past as he drifted onto the shoulder. The passenger in the car shouted something obscene and pitched a beer bottle out the window, then they were around the next bend and gone.

Without showing his teeth, Bobcat grinned at the startled girls and opened the passenger door, Sammy there to greet them with his tail going a mile a minute. One of them was blonde, the other brunette. They were not smiling, and neither made a move to get in.

"Evenin', ladies," Bobcat said, and the brunette said, "What was that all about?" He gave the girls a good-natured shrug and scratched the dog's neck, making its tail go even faster. "Kids," he said. "You know. Maniacs. Good thing you didn't cop a lift with them."

They were trading skeptical looks now and Bobcat knew he'd have to think fast. Either way he wasn't going home empty-handed, but with the late afternoon traffic picking up, he preferred to have this little transaction go smoothly.

The brunette—Laura, he noticed her name inked on the backpack at her feet—opened her mouth to say 'No thanks', and Bobcat said, "Ladies, it's getting late and I got a long way to—"

A transport thundered past in the near lane, rocking the camper, drowning out Bobcat's voice; it was followed by a string of domestic vehicles, most of them towing power boats or campers. In the brief racket Bobcat saw a sticker on the blonde's backpack that said B.C. OR BUST and decided to take the long shot.

When the traffic cleared he said, "I gotta be in Calgary by Wednesday and daylight's wastin'." He emitted a brisk, almost inaudible whistle and Sam hopped into his lap and licked his chin. "You gals coming or not?"

Smiling now, the blonde said, "You're going out West?"

"The Sault tonight," Bobcat said, "then full tilt boogie to the Rockies."

The blonde said, "Can you give us a sec?"

"Take all the time you need."

The girls moved away from the open door, speaking in hushed tones now. Bobcat scratched the dog's ear, pretending he couldn't hear them. But he could. The bobcat had taught how to be still, how to listen."

Blonde: "What do you think?"

Laura: "He's a creep. We should wait for another ride."

Blonde: "Well, I think we should go. We've been standing out here over an hour. It'll be dark soon and I'm getting cold. Besides, look how much that sweet little doggy loves him."

Bobcat kissed the dog on the head. He heard Laura say, "Julie wait," then the blonde was on the running board, sliding in next to him with the backpack on her lap. Bobcat stuck his hand out and the girl shook it, Bobcat saying, "Julie, right?" and the girl nodded. She said, "And my friend's name is—" and Bobcat said, "Laura," and Julie smiled, looking over to see Laura climbing in with a scowl on her face, swinging the door shut behind her.

Bobcat said, "Seatbelts, ladies," and merged into traffic heading north, away from home. The sun was sinking into the trees now, shadows growing longer. He'd have to get this done soon. He didn't like driving at night.

Still on Bobcat's lap, Sammy pushed his head under Julie's arm and the girl scratched his neck and told him how cute he was.

"I just love your dog," she said. "What kind is he?"

"Jack Russell," Bobcat said. "Smartest damn dog in the universe."

Julie said, "This is so freaky. You're really going out West?" and Bobcat drove his elbow into her temple, then reached over and slammed Laura's head against the dash. Both girls slumped over unconscious.

"Not in your lifetime," Bobcat said, slowing to get the rig turned around. "But I have always wanted to see them mountains."

6

Tuesday, June 30

TRISH TOOK OFF right after work, making the drive to Toronto in record time, the Jetta well-behaved for a change. She told her aunt not to expect her much before midnight, and promised to call if she was running any later. She knew Dean wanted to hang out, but she'd had some time to think about it and decided to keep her distance, at least for the time being. The fact that he'd turned his life around was great, for him, but it didn't change anything between them. She'd see him later, pay him back the gas money she'd borrowed and say goodnight.

Her dad's nurse met her in the hall outside the cubicle, and Trish noticed with some pleasure that the name on the door had been changed from *John Doe* to *James Gamble*. The curtains were drawn in there and Trish was eager to go inside.

The nurse said, "He woke up around noon and started trying to get out of bed. Sometimes, when they're in the DTs like this, patients will get fixated on an idea—like getting out of bed—and won't let it go. So we got him up in a chair and that seems to have settled him."

"That's good," Trish said. "Isn't it?"

"Yes and no," the nurse said. "He popped some of his stitches last night and Dr. Peale had to come in and replace them under local. He really should be resting in bed until his wounds heal, but he was so agitated we were afraid he'd tear things loose again. We've got the TV on in there now and that seems to be holding him. But just so you know, if he gets worked up again we may have to ask you to leave."

"I understand. Can I go see him now?"

"Sure. Just let me know if you need anything."

Trish thanked the girl and waited till she left. Then she drew the curtain and went inside.

He was seated with his back to the door, hunched in a padded chair in a chest restraint, a sturdy plastic food tray locked down in front of him, his gaze directed at a small TV in the corner. *The Simpsons* was playing, but Trish couldn't tell if he was watching it or simply staring at the screen. His hands were shaking and a glistening strand of drool hung from his whiskered chin.

Trish said, "Hello," and entered the room, trying not to startle him; but he didn't budge, didn't even look at her.

She moved closer and sank to her haunches beside him, noticing a crude, jailhouse tattoo on his wrist that said *Sal*, and she smiled and touched it with her finger—

Quick as a snake, Jim Gamble spun on her—"Who are you? Where am I? Why am I tied to this fucking chair?"— his ruddy face twisted in fury and bewilderment.

Startled, Trish rose to her full height, saying, "You're in the hospital—"

Last Call

"What *hos*pital? There's nothing wrong with me. *I want the fuck* out *of here!*"

He was trying to lift the tray now, jerking it up and down, trying to squirm out of the chair. Trish looked at the doorway but no one was coming.

He said, "Are you a nurse?"

"No, I'm—"

Then *get* me a nurse, god damn it."

"I'll get you a nurse, but I wanted to tell you...I'm..."

"What? You're what? Get me a nurse, you little cunt. Get me a *nurse. I'm fucking thirsty.*" He seized his IV pole and started wrenching it back and forth, the bags of fluid it supported flapping on their hooks, Jim yelling, *"I need a drink, I need a drink,"* in a mad chorus.

A nurse came in with a paper cup saying, "Okay, Mister Gamble, here's some water," and he batted it out of her hand, splashing everyone in the room. Another nurse appeared with a loaded syringe and asked Trish to wait in the hallway.

Stung, Trish left the unit and took the stairs to the main floor, running full out by the time she hit the lobby. She ran to the Jetta and got in, wondering why she'd even bothered, thinking her mother had been right—he'd called her a *cunt*—determined now to just get on with her new life as a university student. She'd come this far without a dad, she could make it the rest of the way.

When she turned the key the Jetta refused to start and she hammered the dash with her fist, one furious shot that made the radio come on. It was the Power Hour on

CHUM FM and the request line was open, the DJ's manic voice contrasting almost comically with Trish's sobs.

"You're listening to the CHUM FM request line on this sunny Tuesday in June, the last of the month, and this one goes out to Bobcat—yeah, you heard me right, Bobcat—who says he's a dentist and hunting enthusiast. From The Doors..."

The intro to "Light My Fire" came out of the speakers and Trish turned the radio off. She rested her head against the steering wheel for a long beat, thinking, *You can do this, you have to do this,* then grabbed the keys and hurried back inside.

* * *

The madman came through the screen door at the back of the house with a lit Cigarillo in one hand and a portable radio in the other, and Julie cringed as he stomped past her down the steps. He'd locked them overnight in a black box that turned out to be the camper he'd kidnapped them in. Before sunrise he'd dragged Laura into the house and pulled out all of her teeth. Then he'd come back for her.

About an hour ago he'd led them out here, first handcuffing her to the wooden railing at the foot of the steps, then duct-taping Laura to an old vinyl truck seat in the middle of the dirt yard. They were both naked now, shivering is spite of the heat, and there was nothing around them but bush, no other sound but the indolent buzz of cicadas and Laura's helpless sobs. Nearby in a chain-link

Last Call

kennel a half dozen Rottweilers paced in silent agitation, drooling and sniffing the air.

Bobcat set the radio on the bottom step and turned it up loud, grinning at Julie when the announcer said —

"...*goes out to Bobcat — yes, you heard me right, Bobcat — who says he's a dentist and hunting enthusiast. From* The Doors..."

Then "Light My Fire" blared out of the speakers and Bobcat clamped the Cigarillo between his teeth and started Indian dancing around Laura in the yard, bobbing and weaving to the music. Laura gaped at Julie with terror in her eyes.

Bobcat said to Julie, "Now Blondie, I want you to pay attention. I'm thinking I can use you around here a while." He paused behind Laura's back, removing a can of lighter fluid from his hip pocket, and flashed Julie an antic grin, showing those hideous teeth. Then he bit off the cap and spit it to the ground. "But I can't abide no troublemakers."

Julie watched as he resumed his capering, squirting Laura with lighter fluid as he jigged around, making her cry out, the shrill sound provoking the dogs. He made a few more circuits, drenching Laura's shivering body, the yips and howls of the Rottweilers all but drowning out her wretched sobs. He stopped when the can was empty, its contents dripping from Laura's face and breasts and hair.

Looking at Julie, Bobcat said, "This is what happens to troublemakers on the Bobcat ranch." Then he flicked the Cigarillo at Laura, the half-smoked butt snagging in her hair. There was a *!whuff!* of ignition followed by a burst of flame.

Laura's screams, like nothing Julie had ever heard, incensed the dogs even more, and Julie cut her eyes away from the horror in the yard.

Then Bobcat was on her, jerking her head up, making her watch, saying, "Are we clear on this? Blondie?"

"Yes," Julie said. "Oh, God…yes…"

"Well, alright."

Bobcat went back to his manic circling, shaggy head bobbing.

Laura was still now, hunched as if in prayer, engulfed in hell's fire.

* * *

When Trish got back to the unit Jim was still in the chair, his head resting on the food tray now, the sedation working its magic. She pulled up a chair and sat next to him, half-watching a cat food commercial on the tiny TV.

She'd almost dozed off when a familiar voice said, "Wanna take a break?" and she saw Dean standing in the doorway, holding two big bags of Chinese take-out.

She nodded. "Chinese. Smells great."

Her father was still out of it, muttering and snoring, and Trish said, "Be back soon," and followed Dean out of the unit.

They found a vacant couch with a coffee table in the visitors' lounge and Dean opened the bags and doled out the goodies—sweet and sour chicken balls, pork fried rice, won ton soup—all the delicious standards. Suddenly ravenous, Trish dug in.

Once sated, she discarded her plastic fork and said, "What was it like in rehab?"

"For me it was a blessing," Dean said, wiping his mouth on a napkin. "I took to it like a duck to water. The way things were going, I'd likely be dead by now without it. You're thinking about your dad, right? Maybe getting him in?"

Trish nodded. "Do people like him ever make it?"

"I go to three of four recovery meetings a week and I see guys like him all the time. Guys even worse than him with decades of clean time. Anyone can make it if they want it bad enough."

Trish said, "Your offer to help…does it still stand?"

"Of course it does."

Smiling, verging on tears, Trish slid next to him on the couch and gave him a grateful hug.

7

Tuesday, July 14

DEAN STOOD AT the main desk in ICU, trying to persuade the charge nurse, Myrna Sampson, to bend the rules just a fraction. Myrna was a crusty old broad who brooked no nonsense, but Dean had softened her up with a box of Turtles, Myrna's favorite.

"I realize I'm not family," he told her, "but I am a *friend* of the family. And he's going to need a sponsor when he straightens out, someone he can trust. Besides, the exercise'll do him good."

Myrna said, "Alright, you can take him. But I need him back in thirty minutes. We're shipping him out to the floor today and I don't want him tying up the bed."

"Deal," Dean said. "And thanks." He reached over the counter for one of the Turtles and Myrna cracked him on the knuckles with a pen.

Laughing, Dean headed for cubicle 9. Since the night Trish hugged him in the visitors' lounge he'd been paying regular visits to her dad, dropping in every workday for an hour or so. The first few trips had been a waste of time, Jim either deeply sedated or combative as hell; but by the end of that first week his jive-talking street persona had begun to reemerge, giving Dean a glimpse of the man's personality. The six or so days following that had fallen into an amusing pattern, Dean forced to start each new visit from square one, whatever slim progress he'd made the day before lost in the fog of Jim's disease. And today was no different.

"Who are you again, kid?"

They were in the corridor outside the unit now, Jim in hospital-issue slippers and an open-back gown, using his IV pole as a walker, free hand clutching his suture line. To Dean he looked about ready to fold, his stooped frame so skinny Dean could count his ribs through the gown; but he was seeing hints of the toughness in the man now, too, a gleam of purpose coming into those watery eyes. Trouble was, Dean had a pretty good idea of what that purpose was.

"I'm Dean," he said. "Dean Elkind, like I told you before. I'm a friend of a friend. I promised her I'd keep an eye on you."

Jim grunted. "Well, friend of a friend, did I ever tell you about the time we fronted for Aerosmith at the Garden?"

"Only about six times already."

Out of breath now, Jim stopped by a row of chairs and cast his gaze back at the unit, saying, "Listen, kid. Those bitches in there won't let me do shit." He licked his crusty lips. "Why don't you be a sport and run get me a bottle."

"Slim chance of that, gramps."

Jim said, "Yeah, figured you for a company man." He eased himself into one of the chairs, wincing in pain. "How 'bout a deck of smokes, then? You could toddle down to the boutique. I'll wait right here, I promise. Even pay you back, soon as I get through suing these meat packers."

"You'll wait right here?"

Jim grabbed a *Reader's Digest* off a table and crossed his bandy legs. "On this very damn spot, I swear it."

Dean said, "Maybe I'm nuts, but I'm going to trust you. I'll get you some smokes, but I'll hold onto the pack. Once a day I'll take you outside and you can light one up. How's that sound?"

"Peachy," Jim said, grinning, and Dean had to laugh.

"Alright, stay put. I'll be right back."

* * *

Jim Gamble watched the kid scoot out the door into the stairwell, watched the door hiss shut on its piston. He waited—and sure enough there was the kid again, popping his head back in for a final check. Jim waved and said, "Unfiltered Player's'd do it. Make it a large."

The kid grinned and shook his head, and this time when the door latched shut Jim got to his feet and backtracked to a bank of elevators, moving more spryly now, one hand propelling the IV pole, the other pinching his gown shut over his naked ass.

An elevator opened and Jim hustled to catch it, the movement stirring up the rust-colored contents of the catheter bag hooked to the base of the IV pole. Already aboard, an old woman shrank away from him, clutching her purse as he clattered inside. As the doors slid shut,

Jim poked the LOBBY button and rubbed his chapped lips, staring at the numbers above the doors.

In the lobby he set a course for the main exit, but changed his mind when he saw the gorilla-size security guard stationed by the door. He ducked into a side hallway and left the building through a service entrance, stepping out into brilliant sunshine, reflected daylight dazzling him from a hundred polished surfaces. Shading his eyes, he shuffled down the wheelchair ramp to the street, his thirst hard upon him now.

The 4-lane main drag was congested, a long traffic light clogging things up, stretching tempers thin. Jim saw an executive-type step off the curb and almost get clipped by a Transit bus, and he came up behind the guy and said, "Hey, man, can you cut me a break? My law firm went tits up in the last recession and now they got me locked up in here." One of the wheels on his IV pole bumped the guy's shoe and the guy recoiled, storming off in the opposite direction now. Jim tried a couple more passers-by and got the same reaction. He'd given up trying to hide his ass and now people were pointing and smirking.

With nothing on his mind but a drink, Jim wandered into the street, dragging the pole behind him. He tapped on a few car windows without success, then got an inspiration.

He was in the middle of the street now, getting honked and jeered at by angry motorists. Unmindful, he made a beeline for a stationary Honda Civic with an elderly woman at the wheel. Standing by the driver's-side mirror, he plucked the IV bag from its hook, disconnected it from the tubing and squirted the windshield with its salty contents. When the glass was soaked, he set the dribbling bag on the hood and hiked up his gown, baring his balls for the now mortified woman, and started polishing the windscreen with the faded blue fabric.

"There," he said, pressing his face to the smeared glass. "Clean as a whistle. Five bucks oughta cover it."

The light turned green and the Civic surged ahead, leaving Jim with his privates hanging out and traffic whizzing past him on either side. Cursing, parched to the very bone now, he yanked the IV catheter from the back of his hand and abandoned the pole.

A few seconds later traffic was frozen again and Jim glanced into the open interior of the convertible Mercedes that now idled beside him. The driver, a rail-thin platinum blonde, peered at him in mild amusement over the rims of her shades.

But Jim wasn't interested in the woman.

Reading his intent, the woman reached for her purse—a tan leather Chanel on the seat beside her—an instant too late. Jim snatched it up and gave her a grin.

"Thanks, babe, you're a life saver."

Now a police siren warbled nearby and Jim started to move...but then he saw something in the passenger footwell of the Mercedes that gave him pause.

"Oh, mercy me."

He reached into a bag of groceries and came up with a bottle of red wine. Scanning the label in the sunlight, he frowned and said, "This shit for the in-laws?" then moved off down the street, purse in one hand, bottle in the other.

He glanced over his shoulder and saw a city cop and a couple of hospital security guards weaving their way toward him through the traffic.

Running now, the unspeakable pain in his belly all but muted by his thirst, Jim grasped the cork with his teeth and gnawed it free. He glanced back once too often and ran headlong into the grille of an idling semi, dropping the bottle and landing ass first on the scalding pavement. When the bottle shattered by his head, he cried out like a man shot point blank in the spine.

As his pursuers converged, Jim saw an inch of rich red fluid in the unbroken base of the bottle. He picked it up, raised it to his lips—

Then they were on him, one of them knocking the wine out of his trembling fingers. The purse was snatched away and Jim was dragged to his feet. He saw the kid—*Dean, that's his name*—arrive on the scene now, out of breath and scowling, and he shrugged and said, "Hey, kid. You get my smokes?"

* * *

Early the next morning, after another long night of fever dreams and jarring hallucinations, Jim Gamble awoke in the lockdown ward of the mental health unit. He was propped against a mound of pillows on a narrow bed, an invisible jackhammer splitting his skull. He tried to sip water from the paper cup on the overbed tray in front of him and fumbled it, drenching the flannel pajama top he couldn't remember putting on. He said, "Fuck me," and saw a woman with a clipboard on her lap seated in a chair at the foot of the bed. He said, "Pardon my French, sweetheart. I didn't see you there."

The woman said, "I'm not your sweetheart, Mister Gamble, I'm Doctor Kline, the staff psychiatrist assigned to your case."

"Case?" Jim said, thinking how strange it was to hear people using his real name; he'd been CD to so many people for so long, he'd almost forgotten he *had* another name. He said, "The only case I give a shit about has beer in it. Look, lady—doctor—I've got to get out of here, okay? Right now. You have no idea how bad I need a drink."

"I specialize in addiction medicine," Kline said, standing now, tucking the clipboard under her arm. "I know exactly how much you feel like you need a drink."

"You're not reading me, Doc. I don't *feel* like I need a drink, I *need* a drink. You're a bright girl. Med school graduate. Prom queen? Just go get the papers, I'll sign myself out. I've done it before. My belly's fine, see?" He hiked up his soggy pajama top, revealing a raw, jagged scar cross-hatched with suture marks, some of them red and infected looking. "So let's just save everyone a whole lot of grief and get me back on the street where I belong. You can't keep me here—"

"Oh, but that's where you're wrong, Mister Gamble," Kline said. She removed an ominous looking document from her clipboard and held it out for his inspection.

"This is a court order. It entitles me to hold you here indefinitely. That little display you put on in the street yesterday opened a whole can of worms for you, I'm afraid. Something about a series of parole violations and missed court appearances."

"That's bullshit, lady, and you know it."

She placed the document on the tray in front of him. "Here it is in black and white. Bottom line, my friend, I'm going to provide you with some options. I'll lay them out for you in simple terms, then I'm going to introduce you to someone. You'll visit for a while, then I'll come back for your decision. You've been here almost three weeks now. If it hasn't exactly been a Mardi Gras, try to imagine another six months. Or a year. Then maybe we hand you over to the authorities. Are you reading me, Mister Gamble?"

Bitch. "Loud and clear, Doc. Loud and clear."

"Alright, then. Give me a minute."

She left the room and Jim glanced at the document, his fingers itching to rip it to shreds. He felt trapped and hated it; the same way he'd felt in prison. He could never understand why people wouldn't just leave him alone. He'd made up his mind years ago to get high and stay that way, and it was nobody's business whether he lived or—

The doctor came back into the room with a young girl, a stranger in a summer dress. The girl's eyes were shiny, as if she'd been crying or was about to, and her smile quivered on the edge of some emotion Jim was no longer familiar with.

Last Call

Kline said, "Jim, I'd like you to meet your daughter."

Jim said, "My...?" and took a hard look at her, something dawning in a remote recess of his mind. His own eyes growing moist now, he said, "You're Sally's daughter?" and remembered the knife going into his belly, the bald man's smoky breath in his face and thinking, *Please, no...I have a daughter...*

The girl sat on the edge of the bed and took his hand, stilling its tremor. She said, "And yours. I'm your daughter, too."

Jim looked at Kline in open bewilderment.

Smiling, the doctor said, "I'll let you two get acquainted." Then to Jim: "Remember our deal. I'll be back in an hour to discuss your decision."

The doctor left and Jim looked at the girl, a sense of wonder blossoming in his chest. He said, "Trisha?"

"Trish," she said. "How did you know?"

"I came to see you once. The day you were born. I saw you through the big window."

"You saw me?"

Startling Jim, Trish put her arms around him and let her tears come. "Oh, Dad," she said, "I've waited so long..."

Shaken, confused, uncomfortable with this display of emotion, Jim pressed his head against the pillows and blinked at the ceiling, half expecting to see it swarming with bugs, his own eyes filling with tears now.

His hand came up and touched Trish's hair, stroking it awkwardly.

* * *

Trish came out of her father's room holding a wad of tissue. Her eyes were puffy and red, but she was smiling from ear to ear.

Dr. Kline, seated by the door reading a journal, rose to greet her, saying, "So how'd it go?"

"It was great," Trish said, glad now that she'd hung in. "Really great. Now all I've gotta do is figure out how to tell my mother I'll be moving out early."

"So you've decided?"

"Yes. I'll be staying with my aunt in Mississauga and working in her flower shop."

Nodding, Kline said, "Wish me luck, then," and went back into the room.

Trish reclaimed her spot in the chair by the door, feeling the doctor's warmth in the seat, praying her father would take the deal.

* * *

Jim said, "Where I come from, Doc, that's called dirty pool."

"Whatever works," Kline said. "So did it?"

Jim looked out the window at the city below. "I'm not going to promise anything," he said, "but I'll take a shot at treatment."

* * *

Julie landed hard on her back, the drop about fifteen feet to the muddy bottom. Gasping for breath, she watched Bobcat lift the corner of a thick metal plate, the cords in his neck bulging with the strain. Grunting like a boar, he dragged the plate over the mouth of the pit and let it go, the plate dropping into place with a dull thud Julie could feel through the earth.

Bobcat knelt on the plate now, squinting down through one of the air holes, saying, "Can't do nothing right," sounding distracted, mumbling the words as if pulled by other forces. "Feed you to the damn dogs." Then he stood and walked away.

Julie heard the campervan start up, and in a sweep of headlights saw a pair of filthy legs protruding from a shallow tunnel in the wall. In a loud whisper she said, "Hey, you can come out now, he's gone." When she got no response, she poked one of the legs with her finger, then touched it with her palm.

Cold. "Oh, Jesus."

Julie dragged Gail Grafton's body out of the tunnel in the wall. In the scant light she saw the girl's eyes, wide open and clotted with earth, and her toothless mouth, gaping in a sunken face. Her rigor-clawed hands were black from digging, the nails shredded all the way back to the cuticles.

Julie screamed and tried to scale the insloping walls.

* * *

Bobcat sat at the workbench, polishing his treasures with a toothbrush, a lighted mirror on an adjustable arm hovering close by. He was singing a jingle he recalled from childhood...

"You'll wonder where the yellow went, when you brush your teeth with Pep-sodent...Pep-sodent..."

Now he drew the mirror closer and bared his teeth, examining that alarming array of decay interspersed with pearly perfection. With grubby fingers he grasped an incisor that had been giving him grief and tried to wiggle it, but the tooth didn't budge.

"Huh," he said to Sammy, the little guy curled at his feet. "Sucker's in there pretty good."

He grabbed a bottle of Jameson's Irish Whiskey off the bench, chugged back a third and slammed it down hard. Then he picked up the extraction forceps and looked in the mirror. Without hesitation he grasped the incisor and pulled, a growl of perverse stoicism issuing from his throat, rising in intensity as the tooth let go and the Rotties outside yowled in response.

"Mother*fucker*."

He examined the tooth under the work light, fingering its bloody root, then dropped it into an old tobacco tin with a dozen others. Using the mirror, he packed the socket with a pellet of gauze.

While he waited for the socket to dry, Bobcat sorted through the collection of incisors he'd been polishing, five immaculate specimens arranged in a semicircle on the bench in front of him. Nearby on a large square of felt, dozens of other teeth—molars, canines, wisdom teeth—

were arrayed like chess pieces, each of them buffed to a gleaming shine.

Bobcat checked his watch—*seven minutes*—then plucked out the gauze and selected one of the incisors, fitting it into the socket. He appraised the fit in the mirror, then tugged the tooth free and selected another. This new one pleased him and he said, "Sambo, I believe we have a winner."

He removed the incisor—the wet sucking sound reminding him of the time as a boy he lost a sneaker in the bayou mud—dried it with a fresh gauze, then smeared the root with Krazy Glue and inserted it into the socket. He held it there for several seconds, then closed his mouth and ran his tongue over the new addition.

Pleased, he flashed a smile in the mirror, the tooth a perfect fit. Then he turned in his chair to show his result to the room, saying, "What do you think?"

The terrified girl in the torn waitress's uniform wriggled futilely in the barber chair, her bloody mouth already missing half its teeth.

"No opinion?" Bobcat said, standing now. "Well, alright, then. Let's see what else you got."

His shadow fell across her.

8

Friday, July 31

JIM GAMBLE SAID, "Pretty sweet ride you got here, Trish."

Trish glanced over to see if he was pulling her leg, then returned her attention to the road. Following her dad's discharge from TGH this morning they'd grabbed a bite in the cafeteria, then decided to spend a few hours exploring the city, seeing the sights and chatting until his one o'clock appointment at the Webbwood Addictions Center. A few minutes ago Trish had taken a random exit off the Don Valley Parkway and now they were here, in this seamy part of downtown—biker bars, head shops, strip joints—and Trish was worried about running somebody over. Crazy people were everywhere.

In answer, she said, "This old junker? Are you serious?"

"Damn straight. My first car was a Vauxhall Victor I paid fifty bucks for. It had a standard transmission, and the only way I could get it started was to push it down a hill, then jump in and pop the clutch."

Trish laughed, saying, "That sounds pretty bad." The previous Friday a mechanic friend of her mom's had given the Jetta a tune-up and installed a new starter, and now the engine was running like a charm. She said, "Compared to that, I guess it *is* a sweet ride," and smiled, pleased to be spending time with her dad. She'd driven down on three other occasions in the past couple of weeks, just to hang out with him, strolling the streets around the hospital—during one visit he'd given her his version of the fiasco with the stolen bottle of wine, and they'd shared a good laugh over that—or just sitting in his room, shooting the breeze about their lives and their hopes for the future. They were getting to know each other and Trish couldn't be happier, her affection for him growing by the day.

He still looked pretty beat up—his complexion waxy in the daylight, his clothes hanging off his bony frame—but his face was shaven, his long hair combed, and his tremor had all but disappeared. He was wearing jeans today, and a clean shirt buttoned all the way up to the neck.

They were stuck at a red light in front of a biker bar now and a couple of rival club members were having a shouting match in the street. Trish could see that the spectacle was making her dad uncomfortable, and when the light turned green she tramped on the gas pedal, the Jetta laying rubber as they peeled away.

Jim said, "Whoa, there, Mister Andretti," and chuckled.

"Sorry, Dad," Trish said, slowing down. Then: "I guess I should have asked you this before now…but is it okay if I call you 'Dad'?"

Without looking at her, Jim said, "I've been thinking about that, too. How about you just call me 'Jim' until I've earned the title."

Disappointed, Trish said, "Okay, Jim," but she thought she understood.

They were quiet after that and Trish let the silence spin out. There were so many more things she wanted to ask him—and *tell* him—but he was still very sick and she didn't want to upset him. She told herself there'd be plenty of time.

The bars and head shops were turning into restaurants and corner stores now and Jim seemed to be relaxing a little.

Smiling, he said, "You going to give that poor kid Dean another shot? He told me about the shit he pulled, and I'm not saying the booze and the drugs excuse all that, but he has come a long way and I know he regrets it. He's going to sponsor me in the recovery program and—"

"Did he put you up to this?"

"Not at all. Scout's honor. I'm just asking."

"Well, I guess you don't know as much as you think you do, Mister Gamble, because Dean's taking me out to dinner and a movie tonight. Channing Tatum. Who can resist?"

Jim said, "Who's Channing Tatum?" and Trish laughed.

She said, "I feel like doing something outrageous."

"It was that kind of attitude made me the model citizen I am today."

"That's not what I meant…" She spotted a tattoo parlor in a strip mall and pulled in, parking the Jetta out front. "I mean something—*outrageous*. To commemorate our reunion. You know, like a tattoo. I've always wanted another tattoo."

Jim rolled up his sleeves and showed her his arms, saying, "I'm about out of room for tattoos." He said, "*Another* tattoo? Girls do that now? Regular girls, I mean?"

"What do you mean 'regular'?"

"You know. Girls. Who aren't strippers or biker chicks."

Trish laughed. "Everybody's doing it now. It's all the rage."

"Jesus. So where's this tattoo?"

Blushing, Trish untucked her blouse and tugged down the waistband of her jeans, showing him his name rendered in an elegant blue script, low on her hip where her mom couldn't see it.

Squinting, he said, "Is that…?"

"Mm-hmm."

"How…?"

"Your name's on the album."

"When did…?"

The day I turned eighteen." She tucked her shirt back in. "Okay, no more tattoos. Mom'd kill me anyway. How about—"

"Have you told her about me yet? Or about quitting your job at the hotel and moving down here early?"

"I told her about moving."

"How'd she take it?"

"She wasn't happy, but she respects my decision. I'll tell her about you when the time is right—*hey*. Don't change the subject. Out*rage*ous, remember? What about body piercing? Or one of those cool little tooth diamonds?"

Jim said, "I had some trouble in prison with a guy had a nose ring. And I hate dentists."

"Okay, how about this? I'll get the tooth diamond—" She removed a fine gold chain from around her neck and handed it to Jim, letting it curl into the palm of his hand. There was a high school signet ring attached to the chain and when Jim saw it he laughed with pleasure and surprise. Smiling, Trish said, "—and you wear this."

"For Christ sake, is this mine? Where'd you find it?"

"It was in with Mom's stuff."

Trish watched him examine the ring and could almost see the memories filing past behind his eyes, not all of them pleasant. He unclasped the chain and handed it back to her, then slid the ring onto his finger—perfect fit—and smiled.

He said, "You got a deal. But only if you wear this." He took a hand-carved talisman on a leather thong from around his neck and slipped it over her head. "I carved this for your mom in the tenth grade. She...gave it back, and I've been wearing it ever since."

"It's awesome. Thanks, Dad...and you earned that one." She kissed him on the cheek, then got them moving again, leaving the tattoo parlor behind. She said, "Your appointment's not for another two hours. Let's go see what we can find."

* * *

At the Webbwood Addictions Center at 12:55 that afternoon, Jim Gamble sat next to his daughter outside a closed office door with a name plate on it that said, DR. GRAEME LANGTREE, PROGRAM DIRECTOR.

Waiting there in silence with sweat beading on his forehead, Jim felt cornered, ready to bolt, his innate aversion to authority and institutions trying to break loose in him. A familiar inner voice was telling him he could walk out of here right now and vanish into the streets, and that bitch doctor back at TGH, with her legal documents and her pushy deals, could kiss his bony ass right to the red. In his mind, he was already on his feet.

The only thing keeping him here was the girl seated next to him, this sweet, innocent kid who'd had the colossal misfortune of being his child. And even in spite of that, with the clock on the wall ticking off the minutes until that office door opened, it was all he could do not to flee. He couldn't get his knees to stop bouncing, and he didn't believe he'd ever been so thirsty.

Trish took his hand and he almost jumped out of his skin. But his knees stopped moving.

Alright, Jim thought. *Alright.*

At precisely one o'clock, the office door opened and Dr. Langtree appeared, a bear of a man in his fifties with intense green eyes and a ready smile.

"Mister Gamble," he said, and Jim got to his feet. "Come ahead in."

Last Call

As he moved through the doorway, Jim glanced back and saw the sparkle of a tiny diamond in Trish's smile. She said, "I'll be right here when you come out."

Langtree gave her a friendly nod and closed the door.

* * *

The blinds were drawn in here, the light subdued. In a chair off to one side sat a nurse with a clipboard on her knees; she did not look up when Jim came in. On a corner of Langtree's desk stood a cluster of family photos, and on the wall behind it hung a series of framed A.A. slogans: TAKE IT EASY; ONE DAY AT A TIME; FIRST THINGS FIRST. Jim had seen them all before in the Kingston pen, where the warden had tried to force him into the prison recovery program, a misguided attempt at rehabilitation that ended in solitary confinement.

Indicating the chair in front of his desk, Langtree said, "Please, Jim. Sit."

Jim complied, but he could feel the anxiety rearing up again.

Sitting at his desk, the doctor said, "So Jim, why don't you tell us how you came to be with us here today."

Trying for levity, Jim said, "Jesus, Doc, how long've you got?"

"As long as it takes."

Jim looked at his trembling hands, too worn out to pretend anymore. He said, "I've...done some things, Doctor Langtree. Things I never thought too much about until recently. I'm not used to…feeling. I haven't had a drink in a month."

"It's hard," Langtree said. "I understand that. I know exactly how you feel."

Still unable to meet the man's gaze, Jim said, "Excuse me, Doctor. You may know a lot of things, but there's no way you can know how I feel."

"That's where you're wrong, Jim. Six years ago I was sitting right where you are now. In that very chair."

Jim looked into the doctor's eyes for the first time.

Langtree said, "Until six years ago I was a practicing alcoholic and Demerol addict. I was a thoracic surgeon in those days and before I opened a patient's chest I'd sit on the toilet and crank a hundred and fifty milligrams of Demerol into my veins. At night I'd drink myself into a stupor. Seven years ago the College of Physicians and Surgeons revoked my license to practice medicine, the bank took my house and my wife left with my three kids. I spent a year on the street, sleeping in flophouses and puking my guts out on Bay Rum. Believe me, Jim, I know how you feel. You are not alone." He leaned forward in his chair. "There is shame in addiction, Jim. Guilt and shame and constant fear. But there is honor in recovery."

Jim nodded. Absurdly, he felt like crying, the man's words touching something deep and long-forgotten inside of him. He said, "How long will I be here?"

"Six weeks, give or take. Exactly how long will depend on you."

Jim nodded and said, "I took my first drink when I was twelve. Right from the start I had blackouts…"

Last Call

***

Forty minutes later, Langtree shook Jim's hand and the nurse led him to the office door. Trish was standing there when it opened.

Closing the door behind her, the nurse said, "Okay, Mister Gamble, this is where you say goodbye."

Startling him, Trish gave him a warm hug, almost lunging into his arms. The contact felt good and he let it linger; no one had touched him with such innocent affection in a very long time. As she let him go, Jim said, "When you see Dean tonight, thank him for me, would you?"

"I will."

The nurse sniffed and Jim said, "I guess I gotta go. When will I see you again?"

"I have to head back to Sudbury tomorrow," Trish said, "but Stacey's driving down with me next week to help me get set up at Aunt Sadie's." To the nurse she said, "When can I come visit?"

"Not for two weeks," the nurse said. "But there's a family program that runs concurrent with treatment. If you're interested, here's all the information you'll need." She removed a sheath of pamphlets from her clipboard and handed them to Trish. "If you can't attend in person, you can follow along online."

Trish thanked the woman and tucked the pamphlets into her bag. There were tears in her eyes when she said goodbye, and it was all Jim could do to stem the flow of his own.

The nurse led him upstairs to a room with two single beds, a desk and a huge print of a tall ship under sail on a choppy sea. Both beds were neatly made and there was no sign of another patient.

The nurse said, "Take your pick. Get settled in. Orientation's in an hour."

Then she was gone.

Jim sat on the bed by the window and stared out at the grounds, wondering what he was getting himself into, tormented by a thirst that couldn't be quenched.

* * *

Trish and Dean stood on the porch of her aunt Sadie's home in Mississauga, Dean grinning and staring at his shoes. They'd eaten at an exotic East Indian restaurant on Oak Park Boulevard, the cuisine spicy but delicious—not nearly as delicious as Channing Tatum, Trish was quick to point out—and both had been careful to steer the conversation clear of their stormy past. Dean asked how her dad made out at Webbwood and Trish cried a little when she told him.

Now she said, "Thanks for dinner. And the show. I'm a major Channing Tatum fan."

"Yeah," Dean said, still gawking at his shoes. "I got that. Thanks for coming."

On an impulse Trish linked fingers with him and when he raised his eyes she kissed him on the lips. Dean turned bright red and almost fell over, making her laugh. He always could make her laugh. She said, "You've been great through all of this. My dad thinks you're a saint. And I can't tell you how grateful I am that you found him." She kissed him again. "Thanks."

Dean said, "Does this mean you'll go to the Lady Gaga concert with me at the Air Canada Centre next weekend?"

"That's exactly what it means."

He said, "Sure hope I can get tickets, then," and Trish gave him a playful swat. He squeezed her hand then jogged back to his car, a battered old BMW.

* * *

When Dean got home that night, he found Shelley Dixon leaning against his apartment door. He hadn't seen her since the day Trish walked in on them smoking crack in his bed, and as always her delicate beauty disarmed him. She smiled when she saw him, her eyes lighting up, but there was no joy in the expression, only need. At one time he'd believed that yearning was reserved only for him; but he'd learned different over time, and it occurred to him now that he'd do well to remember that. Shelley showing up here now, seven months after he'd broken it off with her and gone into rehab, could only mean one thing. Trouble.

"Hi, doll face," she said, the smile widening as she swept toward him in her low-cut top and micro mini, pressing herself against him now, one firm thigh angling into the V of his crotch. "I've missed you."

She leaned in to kiss him, her scent intoxicating, and Dean turned his face away, feeling the sick heat of her through her clothing, repulsed by it...and yet deeply aroused. She leaned more firmly against him, her smile beckoning now, a tiny moan reverberating in her throat.

Backing her off, Dean said, "Shelley, what are you doing here?" His head was spinning, his mouth bone dry. "I thought we had an understanding. I told you, I don't want to live like this anymore. I can't."

Shelley pushed her bottom lip into a pout, a sad parody of their first weeks together. In those days he would have done anything for her. And did. Blowing every dime he earned, including his savings, keeping her in crack, booze and slinky undies. Shelley had been his dark enchantress, occupying his every thought as she reeled him deeper and deeper into a life of dependency. Looking at her now, it was clear she was in the early stages of withdrawal.

She said, "Come on, Dean, I know you." She slipped a hand into her knitted bag and brought out the crack pipe with the heart-shaped bowl they'd always used, and Dean felt sweat prickling through his scalp at the sight of it. She said, "Let's go inside, okay? I know you're holding. You always shared with me before." That smile, those eyes, undoing him. She said, "We'll do it the way we used to...the pipe in your mouth, your cock in mine..."

Last Call

Dean swallowed hard, his resolve crumbling, and reached into his pocket for his keys. His hand closed around a fold of cash instead and he brought it out—two hundred in twenties he'd grabbed from an ATM on the way home—and now he handed it to her, saying, "Here, take it," and she did, making it disappear. "Now please, Shelley, just go. I'm not holding, I swear. It's like I told you before, I'm done with that life."

But her demeanor had already changed, the girl flush now, eager to score, her ballooning pupils peering into a numb near-future, Shelley saying, "Okay, party poop, be that way if you must." She started away and Dean caught her by the wrist, trying to capture her attention now. He said, "Don't come back here, Shelley, okay?" She nodded, distracted, trying to pull away, and he squeezed her wrist hard enough to make her wince. "I mean it, Shelley. Come back here again and I'll call the cops."

Scowling, furious now, she said, "*Fuck* you, Dean," and pulled away hard as he let her go, Shelley flailing and almost falling to the floor. She got her footing and turned to face him, sticking her wings out like a scrappy hen. "You're an *ass*hole, Dean." He got his keys out and unlocked the door, Shelley saying, "*Dean.* I always hated that name. Dean of what? The college of assholes? I wouldn't suck your dick now if you paid me."

A neighbor down the hall stuck his head out and smirked at Dean, then pulled the door closed.

Dean went inside, Shelley still railing at him out in the hall. As soon as he threw the deadbolt she clammed up, and he could hear her stilettos stabbing the tiles out there now in an eager, receding tattoo.

He leaned against the door and took a shuddering breath, craving the drug and the unhinged sex that had always followed it as ravenously as if he were the one in acute withdrawal.

Then he ran to the toilet and threw up his Indian cuisine, all of it coming in a hot, gagging bolus. When he was done, he filled the sink with cold water and submerged his face in it, still reeling at how close he'd come to letting her in, giving their old dealer a call and embracing the demon, recovery be damned.

He'd come that close.

Heart triphammering, he toweled himself dry and called his sponsor.

* * *

Jim attended his first A.A. meeting that evening in a small gymnasium in the basement of the Webbwood Addictions Centre, joining a sullen group of patients seated in a circle on folding chairs, all of them clutching Styrofoam cups of coffee decanted from a stainless steel urn by the exit. Coffee-Mate dispensers were everywhere. The meeting was presided over by Dr. Langtree, with two burly orderlies stationed at the door.

The woman beside Jim had just finished sharing, telling a version of a story everyone in the room was intimately familiar with, saying how in the early days alcohol had been her best friend, delivering her from a life of loneliness and crippling shyness; but then gradually, over the course of the next twenty years, robbing her of everything but her life, and that only barely. She weighed about ninety pounds, and Jim had seen healthier looking dead people under bridges. He wondered if he looked as bad.

Startling, him, Langtree said, "Jim, I realize this is your first day, but you've seen how Group works, and around here we believe in getting our feet wet right away. So why don't you tell us your story?"

Jim glanced around the circle, seeing only curious, friendly faces, no trace of judgment in their eyes. Many of them reminded him of the people he drank with.

He cleared his throat and said, "In the eighties—"

The woman who'd just shared said, "Hi, my name is…" and Jim said, "Right, sorry. Hi, everyone, my name is Jim and I'm an alcoholic."

The room said, "Hi, Jim," and Jim felt a tiny thrill at the acknowledgement.

He said, "In the eighties I had a rock band. Bad 'n Rude. They were all great musicians, original, dedicated, creative…but I wanted to be Jim Morrison." He said, "When I got drunk enough, I thought I *was* Jim Morrison," and everyone laughed. "We were even born on the same day, Jim and me. December the eighth.

"I was high all the time. At first it worked for me. I played better, sang better, felt better. But before long I started missing cues, forgetting lyrics, embarrassing everyone on stage. Things really started going to hell after the album came out."

Bone tired, his incisions burning like brand iron, Jim leaned forward in his chair and closed his eyes, remembering the night it all ended, a night like so many others before it. There had been label execs in the audience that night and Sally had warned him to take it easy, telling him that if he fucked up tonight she was packing it in for good. He remembered thinking she was just blowing smoke, having threatened the same thing so many times before, and he did what he always did.

He was stoked to the gills before they even hit the stage. Less than two minutes into the opening song, he reached for his bottle of Southern Comfort and tripped over a power cord, falling on his face and snapping the neck off his only guitar, a '59 Les Paul Standard that would have been worth a hundred grand today. He sat there grinning at the stunned audience and Sally threw her arms up and stalked off the stage, saying, "Fuck you, Gamble," as she strode past. "This time it's really over."

He said, "The band broke up after that. It took Sally a couple more years to let me go from her life. She ended up pregnant and I pulled the usual dodges..."

* * *

It was January 18, 1995, the day after the Hanshin earthquake, and Jim was sitting on the couch in front of the TV, rolling a joint and watching news footage of a huge yellow construction vehicle toppling into a fractured roadway in Kobe, Japan. Sally was in the kitchen doing the dishes, dressed in three layers of clothing against the cold in their drafty Spadina Street apartment. She was eight months pregnant.

Jim said, "Sal, you gotta see this," and knocked his beer off the arm of the couch. The bottle spun on the hardwood floor, spewing foam, and Sally came into the room with dish soap dripping from her elbows.

Ignoring the spilled beer, Jim pointed at the screen as he lit the joint, saying, "Lookit this mess," and Sally slapped the joint out of his hand.

"Jesus Christ, Gamble," she said, "will you ever grow up? *Look* at us. We're going to be parents for God's sake. We can't raise a child in this dump. We've got to *do* something. Get it together somehow. Maybe we can go back into the studio, get a decent tour going after the baby comes. My mother said she'd help—"

But Jim wasn't hearing her.

"Shit, Sal," he said, staring at the ruined joint. "That was *Thai* stick. Why're you laying this shit on me, anyways? What makes you think the kid's even mine?"

Tears flashing in her eyes now, Sally said, "That tears it, Gamble," and pointed at the door. "Get the hell out. *Get out.*"

Rattled, Jim righted the beer bottle and retrieved the joint, thinking, *Crazy bitch*. Thinking, *Go to Alfie's for a brew, let her cool off a bit*.

At the door he said, "Can't we talk about this?" and Sally said, "I'm all talked out, Jim. Just stay out of my face, okay? I don't need anymore of your shit."

He pulled on his coat, stepped onto the landing and the door slammed shut behind him, the bolt running home with a snap. He was partway down the stairs when the door opened again and he thought she'd apologize and let him back inside. But Sally flung something that hit him in the face...the burnt-wood Talisman he'd made for her in their teens, the leather thong looping around his ear.

The door slammed again and Jim sat on the steps, thumbing the smooth carving, trying to figure out where he could go. After a while he went outside into the vile January night, shivering in his threadbare coat before he'd walked a city block.

* * *

Jim paused to soothe his throat with a gulp of coffee, the brew chilled now, the group around him silent and attentive. He said, "Nobody wanted any part of me after that. I'd used up all my favors. I hung around the missions for a while, mooching what I could. Then I heard Sally'd had the baby."

He remembered only vaguely the frosty night in February he decided to walk to the hospital from the Salvation Army mission downtown, a two hour trek through a brutal blizzard that all but paralyzed the city. By the time he got there his fingers and toes were frostbitten, and they had to admit him and amputate two of his toes and the tip of his baby finger. But not before he snuck onto the obstetrics ward to see his newborn daughter through the viewing window. He was puking drunk when he got there and within a matter of minutes security was on him, one big bastard putting him in an arm lock and almost ripping his shoulder out of the socket.

But he saw her, plump and healthy, peaceful in the first bassinet by the window, like it was meant to be, the name tag at the foot of the tiny bed saying TRISHA WEST. He remembered feeling stung that Sally had used her last name instead of his, and realized only now how insane that was.

He'd had just those few moments to see her, but a part of him still believed that she had seen him, too.

He said, "I tried to clean up my act after that. Got a job in a sub shop slinging sandwiches. Rented a room in a co-op. But Sally wouldn't let me see our daughter, even after I told her I was clean and had a job, just like she'd always wanted. She said I was right, the kid wasn't mine. Said she'd screwed every guy in the band a dozen times each and had no idea who the father was. I didn't believe her; didn't want to. I hung on for a while, hoping she'd change her mind. But a few months later I was wrecked again."

Around the circle heads were nodding and Jim spoke for another twenty minutes, letting it all come, oddly pleased to be *feeling* again, even if it was only this forgotten breed of pain. And when the meeting ended and everyone stood to recite the Lord's Prayer, he got the strangest feeling he was taller...but then he realized he was really just standing up straight for the first time in too long to remember.

* * *

Bobcat was listening to CHUM FM, tapping his foot to a Hendrix classic while he worked at his bench, the Rotties outside baying and yowling with each burst of the dental drill.

He was wearing his reading glasses now, squinting through an illuminated magnifier with a 16-diopter lens that gave him plenty of magnification but only a 0.5 inch focal length, making it difficult to keep the piece in focus. But it was coming along nicely, maybe his best work yet, like the fat fuck at the trading post was always telling him.

Bobcat was alone tonight, enjoying the quiet—except for those shithounds out there, raising hell every time he ran the drill.

After a few more minutes of buffing he decided the piece was finished, and he admired it through the lens, an intricate carving in miniature of a pair of wildcats flared up in battle. It had taken two large molars to get it done, glued together by the roots to get the limbs entangled.

"My, ain't you the big bad boys. Big bad pussycats."

He removed the piece from its clamp and set it on a jeweler's felt with several others, each depicting a different species of wildcat. Most had already been turned into jewelry he would sell—earrings, charms, amulets—but Bobcat decided right away to add this new one to his trophy necklace as a centerpiece. It was just too damned fine to let go.

Last Call

Using the magnifier, he glued a tiny gold lobster clasp to the head of the dominant cat, and when it dried, added the piece to the center of his necklace, setting it apart with a short length of nylon fishing line. Almost every time he went into the trading post Hank tried to buy the necklace from him, but there was no way he'd ever part with it. There were twenty-nine carvings on it, one from each of his donors so far, only three shy of a full set. The necklace was his pride and joy.

He admired the new addition in the mirror, liking the way the light caught the animals' arched backs, then swiveled his chair to a chest of shallow drawers and slid the top one open. Inside were dozens of teeth, all neatly sorted and aligned.

Finding nothing that appealed to him, Bobcat ran the drawer shut and opened another, equally stocked with human dentition. When he saw one he liked, he mounted it under the magnifier. "Okay, kitty, I can see you already."

He kicked on the pneumatic drill and bent to his work—

But those damned dogs started up again, some of them skirmishing now, driving him batshit crazy, and he swung the magnifier aside.

"Sons of *whores*."

He grabbed his Maglite off the bench, then moved to the back door and threw a switch, bathing the yard in the noon glare of a cluster of Klieg arc lamps mounted on a power pole behind the kennel, startling the dogs and making them cower. Then he stalked into the moonless night, Sammy close on his heels. In the yard he picked up a rock and pelted it at the kennel, scoring a direct hit, one of the Rotties letting out a *yip* of pain.

"Shit factories," Bobcat said and headed for the barn, the dogs even more agitated now. He moved quickly, wanting to get this done, his uneven path lit by the Kliegs.

In the barn he shifted the metal plate and shone the Maglite down the hole, seeing Julie's naked form down there in a fetal curl on a dry platform she'd built for herself out of black earth. He thought, *Clever girl*, and slid an aluminum ladder down the hole, saying, "Watch yourself now, Blondie. Don't wanna bump your noggin with this thing." When the ladder was secure he said, "You come on up now, girl, don't keep me waiting. We got to get you cleaned up and on your way. You're about as useless as tits on a bull and I'm all out of lighter fluid." He chuckled at his own wit. "Come on, now. Don't make me come down there after you."

At first he thought she was dead. Truth was, he'd forgotten about her for a while and hadn't been throwing her any table scraps. Feeding those dogs cost an arm and a leg—and again Bobcat chuckled at his wit—and lately he'd been tossing his dinner scraps to Sammy, the mutt's big Purina feed bag empty. It occurred to him that he'd have to take a run into town soon, grab some dog food and a few groceries. When he got busy with the work like this, the muse running him hard, sometimes weeks went by without him noticing. And when it was really going well, like the twin-molar beauty he'd just finished, well,

Last Call

he barely had the sense to get off the stool and go take a piss.

He said, *"Hey,"* and scuffed dirt into the hole with his boot. "Get your ass up." Thinking that if she was dead he'd have to go down there and carry her up like he did the last one, before she started stinking to the high heaven.

Some of the dirt landed in the girl's face and she stirred.

Relieved, Bobcat said, "Come on now, up you come. Get you shit, showered, shaved and straight the fuck out of here." She was standing now, wobbling on her feet, and Bobcat aimed the flashbeam in her face. "Let's go, Blondie. You've had your fun, now it's time to go. Tell you what, if you're polite, I'll drive you out to the highway. And if you promise not to tell, I might even be persuaded to drop you at the bus station and give you some traveling money. How's that sound?"

She had her arm up shading her eyes, but he saw her nod. He said, "So you promise not to tell?" and she nodded again. "Well, alright, then. Now up you come."

It took her forever, but when she got close enough to grab he caught her by the wrist and dragged her the rest of the way out, saying, "Jesus, girl, you're about as light as a feather. Bobcat's new weight loss program. Results guaran*teed*." He said, "Beats the hell outa Weight Watchers, don't it?" and laughed. It was hard to stay angry when the work was going so well.

She was stumbling all over the place now, falling asleep on her feet. Resisting the urge to belt her, Bobcat pulled the tarp off his snow machine and draped it over her shoulders. He wasn't in the mood for a battle—even in this kind of shape some of these toads could put up one hell of a fight once they saw what was coming—so he coddled her, steadied her as he led her out of the barn, telling her he was sorry things got so out of hand and she'd be sleeping in her own bed tonight, he promised.

He led her to the kennel in the glare of the Klieg lights, saying he had to make sure the gate was locked before he brought her into the house for a shower. The Rottweilers were losing their minds now, barking and brawling, and Bobcat unhooked the cattle prod from the latch post and raked it across the chain-link, the forked tip spewing sparks, and the dogs slunk into the shadows with their tails between their legs.

He opened the gate and flung the girl inside, her thin screams cut short as the dogs bore her down. He went back to the house and stood idle by the screen door for a while, switching the floodlights on and off, first catching glimpses of the brutal frenzy in the kennel, all dust and ribs and surging black dogs; then, in the deep country dark, aware only of the din of savage rending.

When he got bored he returned to his workbench, the dogs quiet now, the new piece already gleaming in his mind.

9

FOR THE BALANCE of that summer, Trish worked in her aunt Sadie's flower shop. She enjoyed the work and the money was great, her aunt paying her thirty bucks an hour cash-money plus a gas card for the Jetta.

Dean visited often, and once near the end of August Trish reciprocated, taking the forty minute drive to Toronto to join him for dinner and a show. She got a bit too tipsy on wine that night to risk the drive home, and Dean was the perfect gentleman, giving up his bed and spending the night on a ratty old couch in the living room. She came dangerously close that night to inviting him into bed with her—and felt a pang of disappointment when he didn't take a shot at it himself—but she could see that he didn't want to rush her. And once she sobered up, she was glad things had worked out the way they did. It occurred to her during the throes of the next morning's hangover that she shouldn't have been drinking in front of a recovering addict in the first place, and she apologized for it later. But Dean just laughed and told her that it was his problem, not hers, and that he wanted her to feel free to be herself whenever they were together. And later, during a hug that morphed into a slow dance on the kitchen floor, he told her that he loved her and that he always had. "And if you think there's still a chance for us,

Trish, I want you to be as sure as you can be before we take things any further." Truth be told, he could have had her right then.

She was on the phone with her dad almost every day. She wanted to visit him at the Center, but he asked her to wait until he was feeling better, saying it embarrassed him to have her see him in such rough shape. Reluctantly, Trish agreed, contenting herself with their phone conversations and the regular news she got from Dean, who as his A.A. sponsor saw him several times a week.

In the middle of August, she made a day trip to the University of Guelph for orientation and to purchase her textbooks, putting a massive hole in her bank account; but for the first time since receiving her letter of acceptance, the future finally felt real to her. She was on her way to becoming a veterinarian, the only thing she'd ever wanted to be. She hoped her dad would be proud of her.

* * *

For Jim, treatment was both a blessing and a curse, each new day a taxing grind of classes and meetings and tormenting thirst. Nights were the worst, frantic using dreams and vivid hallucinations making restful sleep an impossibility.

But in spite of everything, little by little, he was coming back to life. Shaving and showering every day, wearing clean clothes, eating three squares. One day at a time, he was getting better.

Last Call

He admired Dr. Langtree, and in an unexpected, father-son sort of way, found himself wanting to please the man. And whenever he felt like bolting to the nearest liquor store or bar, he remembered their first meeting and the doctor's admission of his own triumph over addiction. Jim had gone into that office expecting to be preached at or bullied and had ended up looking the man square in the eye and returning his honesty. It was a neat goddam trick and it carried over into the A.A. meetings he attended every night, where he found himself actually becoming eager to share. And each time he did, he felt as if he'd shed another small part of some terrible burden he hadn't even realized he'd been carrying. And although he was quick to recognize the benefits of the process, there were many nights he found himself reliving some pretty horrific shit, stuff that, until now, had been lost in a haze of alcohol and narcotics.

* * *

They met every night in the gymnasium, a rag-tag circle of lost souls with downcast eyes guzzling coffee, the majority of them present because they had to be—as a condition of parole or because some governing body had threatened to revoke their license to practice medicine or nursing or dentistry—and a much smaller number because they'd had the shit kicked out of them by their disease and were desperate to find a way out.

On this particular night Jim had decided walking in that when his turn to share came around he was going to pass. He was exhausted, his healing liver ached like a rotten tooth and he just wasn't in the mood for dredging up the past.

Dr. Langtree was chairing the meeting tonight and he must have sensed Jim's unease, because he corralled him at the coffee urn and asked him to read the A.A. Promises during the preamble. Jim almost refused, but didn't want to appear rude.

Imagine that, he thought, accepting the laminated card with the Promises listed on it. *Not bad for a guy who just a few weeks ago thought nothing of shitting himself on a Transit bus.*

And goddammit, as he read the Promises aloud he began to feel better, as if he were a part of something now and the words he was reading held some truth for *him*. He could see Dr. Langtree smiling with pride.

In a full voice, Jim said, "The A.A. Promises. One: If we are painstaking about this phase of our recovery, we will be amazed before we are halfway through. Two: We are going to know a new freedom and a new happiness. Three: We will not regret the past nor wish to shut the door on it…"

And when the preamble ended and Jim's turn to share came around, Dr. Langtree said, "Jim, last time you were telling us about life on the street. Feel like picking up where you left off?"

Jim said, "Yeah, sure, the street. I adapted quickly. I guess I had a knack for the lifestyle. I was a liar and a con and, thanks to my father, pretty handy with my fists."

Last Call

A heavily tattooed teenage girl seated across from him said, "Your father beat you?" and Jim said, "Naw, he paid for boxing lessons." He said, "For a while in my teens I wanted to be Muhammad Ali," and a few people laughed. "I got pretty good at it, too. And it served me well on the street, depending on how shitfaced I was at the time. I had the crap beat out of me dozens of times. Spent a month in the hospital after one episode, two weeks of that in a coma. But mostly I fared pretty well. This one night I got into it with these two bums tried to roll me for a bottle..."

* * *

He'd seen these two douchebags before, big-gutted bullies in filthy twill shirts, rousting people from their hovels and boosting their shit, and there was no *way* they were getting his bottle. He'd worked all day to acquire it, and as soon as he was done crippling these pricks he was gonna sit his ass down by the trash fire over there and drain the sucker dry.

He set the bottle of Mad Dog 20/20 on the ground by the overpass wall and picked up a length of two-by-four he kept handy for the edification of assholes like these. They were almost on him now, acting all cool like they were just moseying over for a chat. *Dipshits.*

The first one, the guy with the wizard's beard, said, "You're CD, right?"

"Who wants to know?"

The other guy, this one wearing aviator shades in the dark, said, "What's the plank for, buddy? You building a house?"

Both of them laughed. They were closing in now, flanking him like jackals, fat fists coming out of empty pockets to hang ready at their sides.

Jim said, "I use it for dance lessons," and clipped the bearded guy on the knee, sending him hopping off in pain. The second guy kept coming and Jim feinted with the two-by-four and kicked him in the balls. The guy went down hard and Jim was on him, mashing the sunglasses into his face with the butt end of the board.

"You shitheads wanna steal from me? Well, bring it on, bitches, bring it *on*."

* * *

Jim said, "Something came loose in me that night. If the cops hadn't shown up when they did, I would've killed that guy."

Around the circle heads were nodding.

"I developed a taste for codeine on the street. This one night me and my buddy DelRay broke into a drug store downtown. The owners lived upstairs and called the cops. We got busted going out the door. DelRay tried to run and they shot him in the leg. I got tied to a string of other robberies and ended up serving three years in the Kingston pen. That's where I met my mistress. Heroin."

Jim had an unfamiliar sensation then. *Is it shame?* Stymied by it, he said, "Anyways, I did my time and they put me back on the street. After that—"

Langtree said, "Jim, before you go on, why don't you share your experience in prison?"

Jim put his head down. There was that feeling again. He said, "I don't think I want to talk about that."

"This is your third week here, Jim," Langtree said. "As recovering addicts, the parts of our lives that have caused us the most pain are precisely the parts we must purge. This is the place to do that. So please, share with us."

Jim kept his gaze on his lap and shook his head.

Langtree said, "I think the group deserves—" and Jim said, "Why are you pushing me, man?" Looking up now, fists clenched. "I told you I don't want to talk about it."

"I understand that," Langtree said, not letting it go, "but—"

Shaking his head, Jim said, "To hell with this," and stormed out of the room, thinking, *I told you I don't want to talk about that shit. Are you* deaf? On his way out he heard the scrape of a chair, someone getting up to follow him, then heard Langtree say, "No. Let him go."

He slammed the gymnasium door and bounded up the stairs to his room, his healing incisions punishing him for it. Thirstier than he'd ever been, he stuffed his few belongings into a pillowcase, his mind racing ahead to the pub two short blocks away, his practiced fingers counting out the change in his pocket, not enough to get him all the way there but enough to take the edge off. *Stick this place up your arse,* Lang*tree. What kind of fucked up name is that, anyway?*

Then he saw the strip of black & white photos he and Trish had taken in a photo booth the day she got her tooth diamond; the day she dropped him off here. He picked it up and studied each frame in the lamp light, the two of them crammed into that tiny booth, making faces and acting the fool.

Rubbing his parched lips, Jim set the pillowcase on a chair and stretched out on the bed with his shoes on. With a tortured sigh, he closed his eyes and slept through the night for the first time since his teens.

At some point in the dark reaches of that night, curled now from the warmth of Jim's hand, the photos tumbled off his chest to the floor.

* * *

The next evening, Jim got a call from Trish, the few other patients he'd gotten close to over the weeks ribbing him about the big ol' grin on his face as he hustled to the booth to take it.

She sounded tired, saying, "How's it going? How do you feel?"

He wanted to tell her everything was great, not make her worry, but before he could stop himself he said, "It's hard, Trish. Everybody poking at you, wanting inside your head. And I get so damn thirsty sometimes it's all I can think about. They tell me if I'm going to make it, I've got to do it for myself." He felt his face flush. "So far I've been trying to do it for you."

There was a beat of silence then and Jim thought she might be crying. He thought, *You're an asshole, Gamble*, and said, "I'm sorry, you know. For leaving you. I've got no excuse. I did it. Nobody made me. But I am sorry."

"I know that, Jim."

Hesitating, he said, "If you still want to, you can call me 'Dad'. I'd like you to."

Now she was crying. "I want to. I've always wanted to. In the Family Program they talk about letting go of the past, learning to live in today. Why don't we concentrate on that? I forgave you a long time ago. And if the only way you can stay sober right now is to do it for me, then do it that way. Fake it till you make it, isn't that what they say? In time, you'll find reasons of your own."

Smiling, tearing up now himself, Jim said, "You're just like your mom, you know it?"

Trish laughed. "I'm not so sure that's a compliment."

"I hear you. She's got her rough side. But if she loves you she'd die for you and that's not something you find every day."

"I know. I love her like crazy, too."

A nurse was waving him out of the phone booth now, pointing at her watch. Jim nodded and said, "Trish, I gotta go. Our recovery meeting's early tonight 'cause Doctor Langtree's giving a lecture later in the auditorium."

"Okay. I love you, Dad. Same time tomorrow?"

I love you, Dad. It was the first time she'd said it to him.

"I love you, too," he said. "Same time tomorrow."

* * *

Once the preamble was done, Langtree centered him out right away. "I'm going to start with you tonight, Jim. I think we should pick up where we left off last time. I'd like you to tell us about your experience in prison. You're welcome to leave again, but I have to warn you: If you do, you won't be invited to return."

No proud smile tonight.

Still glowing from his chat with Trish, Jim said, "I was scared shitless. All I knew about federal prison was what I'd seen in the movies." He looked at Langtree and saw him nod. "In some ways it was like the street. But mostly it was pure jungle. As soon as you walked in you became part of the food chain.

"I got on the wrong side of this guy…"

* * *

It was late October and a greasy snow was falling, turning the yard into a slippery hog wallow. Jim was leaning against the fence smoking a rolly-o when a muddy soccer ball came out of nowhere and smacked him in the face, ruining his cigarette and making his nose bleed.

A muscle-head with a nose ring charged over and pinned him to the chain-link, his thick forearm crushing

Jim's voice box. One of his confederates ran up with the soccer ball saying, "Hey, Terry, lookit this."

Terry looked at the ball, then back at Jim. He said, "You got blood on my ball," then cocked his head quizzically, like a dog watching a squirrel circle a tree. He said, "You work in the kitchen, right? Washin' pots?" He looked at the dimwit with the soccer ball. "That's where I seen this jackoff before, right, Woody?" Woody nodded, saying, "Potsy," and Terry said, "Good one," returning his dull gaze to Jim, the two of them close enough now to kiss. He said, "From now on, fuck face, that's your new name. Potsy." He pressed a finger to Jim's lips, two other muscle-bound psychos closing in now, Terry saying, "Nice pie-hole you got there, Potsy." Grinning, showing some really bad teeth. "I just figured out how you can make it up to me."

Jim thought, *Fuck this*, tensed to knee the guy in the nuts and run like hell—and a guard broke it up.

Strutting away, October frost on his foul breath, Terry grabbed his crotch and said, "You look like a meat eater to me, Potsy. I like it right after supper. You see me right after supper, hear?"

***

Jim said, "They came for me in the kitchen. Three of them. I knew I couldn't fight them all, but I had to try. A lot of wretched shit happened after that night, but I've never been as scared as I was in that moment."

* * *

Terry, Woody, and another yard ape, this one tattooed over every visible inch of skin including his face, came up on him at the pot sink. Without a word or a glance, the other two guys working cleanup left the area at a quick march. Jim said, "Thanks, guys," to their backs and picked up an iron skillet.

Terry said, "I told you to see me after supper, Potsy. I told you that's when I like my head." Jim brandished the skillet and Terry chuckled, saying, "You gonna smack me with that, Potsy? Go ahead, give it your best—"

Jim swung the heavy skillet with everything he had. Cat quick, Terry stepped inside the attack and plucked the skillet out of his hand, in the same smooth motion tapping Jim on the head with it, dazing him.

"Hold 'im," Terry said, tossing the skillet into the sink. "On his knees."

The other two forced Jim to his knees on the greasy tiles. Terry unzipped his trousers.

"Grab his face. Open that honey hole."

Seeing stars, Jim said, "Put that thing in my mouth, I bite it off."

Terry kicked him in the belly hard enough to make him retch. Gasping for breath, Jim said, "Bite…it…" He bared his teeth and clicked them together, grinning now, saying, "Right…the fuck…off." Now that he was in the situation and they'd hurt him physically, a lot of the fear drained away.

Terry studied him a moment, then said, "Alright, flip him over."

The two cronies dragged him to his feet and doubled him over the sink, one of them dunking his face into the soapy water. Terry yanked Jim's pants down and grabbed him by the hips.

"Now hold him steady," Terry said. "If he fights, drown him. Fucking virgins, always talkin' about biting."

The three men laughed.

Then Jim felt the man inside him and heard the ring of his own screams in the stainless steel kitchen. By the time the last of them got through with him, Jim had sworn he'd kill them all. But he never did.

They left him there with his pants around his ankles, blood drizzling his thighs, the three of them talking about watching the game on the tube tonight, Terry saying god help any stupid son of a whore who tried to change the channel.

***

You could hear a pin drop in the gymnasium, the circle of listeners a frozen tableau. A few of the women had tears in their eyes. Jim did, too.

He said, "The next time they came after me they hit me up with heroin first. Within a week I was going around to the bastard's cell, begging for more. I was a junkie from my first taste. I...did things with him...to him. For the junk. Things I'm so...."

But he couldn't go on. He looked at Langtree and said, "Happy now?"

"Of course I'm not happy," Langtree said. "But I am very proud. That took real courage, Jim, the kind of courage it takes to leave this place at the end of your stay and live a clean, productive life on the outside. The sad truth is, relapse rates for alcohol and narcotics are extremely high, greater than sixty percent in even the most motivated patients. But based on what you've accomplished here tonight, I'd say if anyone's got a chance of beating those odds, it's you."

A tinkle of applause grew to a roar that echoed off the stark gymnasium walls, and for the first time since coming here — maybe for the first time in his adult life — Jim felt as if he might just have a chance.

* * *

At 9:00 o'clock on the morning of August 10th, six weeks to the day following his admission to Webbwood, Jim Gamble sat across from Dr. Langtree with his hands folded in his lap and a knapsack containing his few belongings resting on the floor between his feet. Unlike his initial visit to the doctor's office, the blinds were wide open today and the room was filled with morning sunshine. There was no silent nurse sitting in the corner with a clipboard on her knees, and Jim felt better than he had in decades.

Smiling, Langtree said, "Well, Jim, how does it feel to be leaving?"

"Scary as hell."

The doctor laughed. "That's a pretty normal reaction. It'll pass. All set up at the halfway house?"

"Yep. Got a room with a view."

"Job search pan out?"

"No, nothing yet."

Nodding, Langtree said, "All in due course," and got to his feet. Jim followed suit, slinging the knapsack over his shoulder.

"You've done well here, Jim," Langtree said. "But a word of caution. Outside, there'll be no one looking over your shoulder. No one to hold you accountable. So use what you've learned in Program. Go to meetings, as many as you can. Use your sponsor; Dean's a good kid who's successfully tackling a brutal addiction. Read your Big Book—and don't take that first drink. You can do it, Jim. One day at a time, you can do it."

Langtree came around the desk and the men shook hands.

"Thanks, Doctor Langtree," Jim said. "Thank you very much for everything."

Feeling absurdly like he was being thrown to the wolves, Jim left the office and exited the building by the main entrance, digging his bus pass out of his pocket and wondering what he should do next. Surprising him, Trish and Dean popped up all smiles from behind a bordering hedge. With tears in his eyes Jim accepted their congratulatory hugs and remembered something Langtree had told him that first day in his office: *You are not alone.*

Grinning, Jim said, "Alright, who wants to go drinking?" and they all shared a good laugh.

"Okay," Dean said, taking Trish's hand. "Let's go check out your new crib."

* * *

One late night in the last week of October, Sally West came out of the Radisson Hotel at the end of her shift and stood on the sidewalk in the autumn chill, shivering and thinking she could use a drink. There was a perfectly nice bar in the hotel, but she'd just spent the past twelve hours working her tail off in there and decided she'd had enough of the place for one day. She could go home and get a glow on in comfort—run a hot bath, float a nice Merlot in the water with her and sip it straight out of the bottle—but the thought of spending another night alone in that house was just too depressing.

She stepped off the curb and headed for the parking lot, checking her watch as she went: 12:01 A.M. on a Friday night. *Huh.* Pushing forty, all dressed up in her work clothes smelling of hotel confections, and no place to go.

She missed Trish very much.

But the kid was doing great down in Guelph, managing the hefty course load like a pro, working weekends in Sadie's shop and gabbing with her old lady every night on the phone. She hadn't been home for a visit yet, but Sally understood; it was a five hour drive, gas was expensive, and she had to grab as much study time as she could.

Last Call

Sally got in the car, keyed the ignition and belted herself in—then she fished the cell phone out of her purse and turned it on, scrolling through her contacts to Trish's number. She didn't have anything to say, really, she just wanted to hear the kid's voice; right now, she wanted that more than anything else in the world.

She touched the screen, making the connection—then cut it off before it had a chance to ring. It was after midnight and Trish would be sleeping, Sadie expecting her in the shop before 8:00 A.M. on Saturdays.

Sally returned the phone to her purse and started crying, just like that, the tears coming quick and hot and insistent. She hated behaving like this, had always seen it as a sign of weakness; but whatever this was, it was clear she was just going to have to ride it out.

She turned on the radio and snatched a wad of Kleenex out of the glove box, Q92 playing some bluesy oldies tonight as she dabbed her eyes, Zeppelin's "Stairway to Heaven," sliding smoothly into "Desperado," by the Eagles.

The song reminded her of her gigging days and how much she'd loved that feeling, getting up on stage wearing sassy-ass shit she'd never have been caught dead in anywhere else, using her sexuality and her passion for the music to knock the audience *out*. Bad 'n Rude. It was Gamble who'd come up with that name, and it had fit them like a glove. They'd done mostly classic rock covers in their live show, and "Desperado" had been one of Sally's favorites, but the Linda Rondstat version, not The Eagles'. In those days reviewers had compared her to

Rondstat, calling her a refreshing cross between Linda and k.d. lang, with a pinch of Joplin thrown in for good measure. Man, did she miss those times.

Sally thought, *Shit*, the tears coming even harder now, *this isn't helping*, and she shut the radio off. Then she dried her eyes, put the car in gear and got the hell out of the parking lot.

She got stuck at a red light on Paris Street downtown, a thin drizzle falling now, and absently noticed a bright yellow 60s-style poster taped to a light stanchion on the median—*Open Mic Night at The Townhouse, Midnight to 2 A.M.*—with today's date on it. By the time the light turned green, the information had left her mind; but two blocks later she turned right onto Elgin Street and found a parking spot directly in front of the bar.

She got out in the rain in her square, businesswoman's suit and went inside like she belonged there, drawing stares from the youthful patrons as she strode to the edge of the stage and caught the bass player's attention. She shouted her request to the guy—there was a heavily-tattooed girl of about Trish's age at the mic now, performing some kind of death metal massacre on a Michael Jackson tune—and the bass player nodded gratefully and turned to the band, abruptly ending the song. The screamo kid gave Sally a dirty look, her mousy face so full of piercings it looked like an open tackle box, then stormed off to the ladies' room.

Before she could stop herself, Sally stepped onto the low stage and stood at the mic, undoing the top two buttons of her sensible blouse. Now the bass player—a very tall, very thin guy in his mid-thirties with gentle eyes and a ready smile—said, "Shall we call you 'Supervisor' or do you have a name?" Smiling, Sally glanced at the embroidered title on her breast pocket and slipped the jacket off, letting it puddle on the stage in front of the bass drum. She said, "Call me 'Sal'." Then: "Do you guys know "Desperado"?" and the bass player nodded, saying, "I'm guessing the Rondstat version?" and Sally said, "The very one."

She faced the crowd as the bass player introduced her and the drummer counted it in. And when the keyboard player struck those first sweet chords, Sally felt the tears coming again...but she closed her eyes and locked that sadness in, slipping a harness over it, waiting for her cue.

She hadn't sung a note in over a decade.

But when that exquisite moment of pause came, the last note of the intro fading into the expectant silence, Sally opened her mouth and sang those four iconic syllables as if her last gig had been only yesterday. And although she couldn't hear it, she could *feel* the room gasp—the hip kids in the audience, the waitresses and the barkeep, the musicians behind her—every last one of them with their eyes on her now, and Sally felt the excitement effervesce out of the domes of her shoulders into the back of her neck and she knew, just *knew*, that everyone else did, too.

She sang the song with everything she was and everything she'd ever been, and when the tears got away on her again she failed to notice. She plucked the mic off the stand and simply stood there, letting it come in the effortless way it always had, making eye contact with everyone in turn.

When she was done there was only silence, and Sally got the shrinking feeling she'd bombed and that she'd best just go home, drink herself to sleep in the tub and pray for a peaceful drowning.

Then the place erupted in applause, and the thirty or so kids at the tables got to their feet and started chanting, *"Do one more, do one more,"* and Sally dried her eyes on her sleeve and asked the band if they knew "Whole Lotta Love".

* * *

On the afternoon the first snowflakes sifted out of the November overcast, Bobcat moved the campervan into the barn for the season, parking it over the hole in the ground—empty now, the last of his guests dispatched—and covering it with a huge tarpaulin. Winters up here were harsh and long, and something about that kind of weather soured his taste for the hunt. He'd use his old Chevy pickup until spring, when the urge would surface again and he'd return to his usual haunts.

For now, though, he had enough raw materials to carry him through the season, and sufficient pre-orders to keep the bills paid and the pantry well stocked. And if he did run out, well, bovine teeth would do in a pinch, and there were cattle farms all over the place around here. A rip-off, granted—there was just something about the texture of human dentition that made it ideally suited to the craft—but sometimes you just did what you had to do. The dogs he'd feed the big ten-point buck he'd shot out of season, the animal already butchered and stored in two big freezers in the summer kitchen, along with the remains of a pregnant moose he'd found dead on the highway, clipped by a passing trucker. And if that wasn't enough for the yappy fuckers, they could starve to death.

He was almost ready to settle in. Hibernate like the big ol' bear that he was. The thought made him grin. He backed the Chevy out of the barn and climbed down to check the tread on the snow tires.

Until six years ago, when his ma died and he got the Rotties, Bobcat had packed up the camper and headed south for the winter, spending those five long months back home on the bayou outside of St. Francisville, Louisiana. He still owned the property down there—under his real name, Anatole Amos Polk—but without his ma there to take care of the place it was just a shack, and it could burn to the ground for all he cared. He hadn't been back since the funeral, and reckoned the place was probably overrun with rats and coons by now. Or maybe one of the beer-gutted, redneck swampers his ma used to entertain had turned it into a whorehouse. Either way, he could give a shit. Nothing but bad memories back there, people calling him a freak on account of his malformed ears and some of his toes being fused, calling him a snaggle-toothed tree monkey, every ugly thing they could think of.

And the worst of them was his own ma, the sow, nothing ever good enough. He could only remember her ever hugging him once in his lifetime, the day he killed the copperhead that got into her shower stall, chopping it's head off with a garden hoe. And even that felt more like he was just something handy to grab hold of than it did a hug. That last winter he'd spent with her down there he'd pretty much decided that if she was still alive the following year, he'd slit her wattled throat just like he had his daddy's and sink her next to that mean old bastard in the swamp.

Bobcat drove the pickup into the backyard and parked it by the kennel, feeling bitter now, these unbidden thoughts of his dark days back home making him want to kill something. Compounding his misery, the molar that had been giving him grief was starting to act up again.

When he got out of the truck, one of the Rotties—the big alpha male with the star-shaped marking on its chest—gave him a dirty look, trying to stare him down, and Bobcat thought, *I'm gonna blow your brains out and feed your balls to your cellmates*, but by the time he got to the closet where he kept the rifle it was the toothache that had his full attention. Forgoing the gun, he dug the whisky out of the pantry, the forceps and the Krazy Glue off the workbench and settled in for the task at hand. He hoped he had a decent match in his collection.

It was going to be a long damn winter.

* * *

Last Call

On the evening of Monday, February sixteenth, Jim and Dean attended an A.A. meeting together, then drove to Dean's apartment. It was Trish's twenty-first birthday and they wanted to surprise her with a Skype call, the two of them donning pointy party hats and clamping dollar-store blowouts between their teeth, ready to blast them at the screen when Trish came online. They knew that her mother had driven down from Sudbury to spend the weekend with her, and that she was supposed to have left yesterday, but at the last minute Jim decided to stay out of sight until they were certain Sally was gone. Trish hadn't told her about him yet, and he didn't want to blow it for her by getting caught on her computer screen.

When Trish came online Dean said, "Are you alone?" and when she said, "Yes," both men stuck their faces into the screen and honked their blowouts, having a sword fight with them now and acting the fool, then they sang "Happy Birthday". Trish smiled and said, "It's about time you guys called; I was beginning to think you'd forgotten." Playful, but letting them know it mattered.

They chatted for a while about life and school and the many wonders of Kraft Dinner, then Jim told Trish he had a job interview coming up later in the week, an opportunity Dean had found for him with the support staff at TGH. Trish said that was great and wished him luck, then told them about a little confession her mother had made during her birthday visit.

"She's in a band now," Trish said and Jim laughed, saying, "Man, that's great," genuinely pleased for her.

Trish said, "It's a group of young Laurentian University professors," and told them how Sally had inadvertently auditioned for the lead singer slot back in October. She said, "They call themselves 'Summa cum Loudly'," and Dean chuckled at the academic pun. "Weekend warriors, Mom calls them. But they're really talented, and Mom sounds amazing. I'll send you a link to a YouTube video somebody posted." Trish giggled. "Wait'll you see what she's wearing; very cheeky. I asked her why she waited so long to tell me about it and she said she didn't want to bring it up until she was sure she wanted to go through with it. They're just playing the club scene right now, but Mom says they've got enough original material for an EP, so they're going to launch a Kickstarter campaign in the spring and see what happens."

They chatted and goofed around for over an hour, then signed off, Trish saying she had an Anatomy quiz in the morning. After a quick cup of coffee, Dean drove Jim home in the opening salvo of the worst blizzard to hit the city in over fifty years.

FOUR MONTHS LATER

10

Monday, June 27

TRISH SAID, "YEAH, Dad, she looks great. Not a day over thirty."

On the other end of the line in Toronto Jim said, "Did you punk her yet?"

Trish laughed and pressed the phone closer to her ear, old peoples' dance music and raised voices from the living room making it difficult to hear. She moved from the hallway into the kitchen saying, "Forty pink flamingos on the front lawn. She nearly shit. Kicked a hole in one of 'em."

"That sounds like Sally. Was Dean able to join you up in Sudbury?"

"He had to work."

"Still think you can make it in the morning?"

"Count on it, Dad. It's your one-year anniversary. I wouldn't miss it for the world—oh, hold on."

Sally came into the kitchen now with a much younger man in tow; they were both pretty bombed. She said to Trish, "Who are you gabbing with now?"

"Dean," Trish lied; she'd been doing a lot of that in the past twelve months.

"Well, come on, party poop, tell him you gotta go. It's time to cut the cake."

Sally got a slicing knife out of the utensil drawer, then swapped a wet kiss with her suitor. When they broke, she wagged the knife at him, saying, "From the Bobbitt line— and I know how to use it." The two of them giggled and weaved back into the living room.

Trish said, "Sorry, Dad. Mom's having a midlife crisis. My alarm's set for five-thirty. Don't worry, I'll be there in plenty of time."

Now Stacey be-bopped into the kitchen saying, "Will you for Christ-sake come *on*," and Trish said, "Dad, I gotta go. I'll see you at the meeting in the morning, ten-thirty sharp. I'm so *proud* of you."

"Thanks, kid. Drive safe."

Trish said she would, then signed off and followed Stacey into the living room, where a dozen people stood around a huge chocolate cake blazing with candles. The group broke into a drunken chorus of "Happy Birthday", then Sally handed the knife to Trish, saying, "Here, little sister. This was your idea, you cut the cake."

Trish took the knife and pressed the blade into the cake. She fumbled the first piece lifting it out and now she jerked her hand away, dropping the slice to the floor. A bead of blood appeared on her baby finger and she popped it into her mouth, grimacing in pain.

Her mother took her by the wrist. "Here, let me see." Trish showed her and Sally said, "Oh, my God, somebody call nine-one-one."

"Very funny, Mom. It *hurts*."

Sally rolled her eyes and led her daughter into the kitchen. Trish hopped onto the counter by the sink, where her mother had patched countless nicks and scrapes over the years, and held out her finger for repair. Sally wrapped a band aid around the cut, then kissed the tip of Trish's finger. To finish the job, she drew a tiny heart on the band aid with a ballpoint pen.

"There you go, kitten. I think you're gonna live."

"Thanks, Mom. Happy Birthday."

They smiled at each other and embraced. After a long moment Trish pushed her mother away, saying, "You smell like a brewery," and hopped to the floor. "Let's eat cake."

* * *

Trish begged off to bed after dessert, telling her mom she had to leave early in the morning to do some inventory at the flower shop. Another lie. Her aunt Sadie said she'd cover for her if her mother asked, but told her she was getting tired of lying and felt it was high time Trish told her mom the truth about her dad. He'd been clean and sober for a year now, Sadie said, and he seemed determined to stay that way. She said they both knew that even if Jim became a missionary and saved a thousand souls a day, Trish was still going to catch hell for going behind her mother's back, so what was the point in putting it off any longer? Better to just get it over with.

Trish agreed, promising she'd get it done right after her dad's anniversary celebration. She'd tell her mom tomorrow. Over the phone. From a safe distance. Say, four hundred kilometers away.

She turned off the light and snuggled under her comforter, the muted sounds of music and merriment from downstairs lulling her into a dreamless slumber.

* * *

Trish awoke ahead of the alarm, showered and dressed quickly, then got her dad's anniversary gift out from under the bed, a Gibson Hummingbird acoustic guitar with a big red ribbon tied in a bow around the neck. The guitar was used and had a superficial crack in the top, but she'd picked it up for a steal from an elderly neighbor whose arthritis made it impossible for him to play anymore. "Take it," he told her, "and give it a good home. Lots of memories in that thing."

Now, creeping down the stairs to make good her escape, Trish thought, *We'll be making all new memories with it soon.*

The main floor was a disaster area, empty wine bottles, beer cans and chip bags scattered everywhere, her mom and the young stud passed out in a tangle on the couch—fully dressed, thank God—and Trish saw another couple sandwiched into the old leather La-Z-Boy in front of the TV, which was turned on but muted, tuned to a Dr. Ho infomercial. There was no sign of Stacey.

Trish wanted to eat something before she left, but now her mother opened her eyes and looked right at her...then yawned and went back to sleep. Not wanting to have to explain the guitar, Trish crept out the front door and locked it behind her, deciding she'd grab a quick bite on the road.

She stowed the guitar in the back seat of the Jetta, sat behind the wheel and turned the key.

Whiz!

"Oh, shit, no. Not today. When we get to Toronto you can explode, but please…"

She turned the key again and the engine started. The radio came on—ZZ Top's "La Grange"—and Trish smiled and backed out of the driveway.

* * *

Bobcat nursed a coffee in a window booth at his favorite trolling spot, clocking the busy parking lot through the bug-specked glass. He preferred his usual perch against the railing, but earlier this morning a kid in a puke-green uniform had come out and told him he couldn't loiter there any longer. Safety regulations, the kid said. Bobcat thought, *If the little shit only knew*, and chuckled under his breath.

Today was only his third hunt this season, after a six-month run of feverish work, the most productive stretch he'd ever had. Last fall Hank at the trading post had talked him into expanding into the online marketplace, and Bobcat had been working twelve hours a day ever since just trying to keep up, cranking out some quality pieces and burning through the bulk of his inventory.

He needed something special today to finish off a bracelet that would net him over a grand. Trouble was, the breakfast crowd was just one waddling, buck-toothed fat fuck after another. It was a goddam shame. When he was a kid in Louisiana you had to pay two bits at a freak tent to see mutants like these and now they were everywhere, lined up at coffee shops and donut shops and supermarkets, stuffing their doughy faces. Toronto was crawling with them. If the city ever got nuked, he sometimes mused, there'd be a hundred-year grease fire—

An older model brown Jetta pulled into the lot, its image reflected in the window glass, and Bobcat felt a twinge of familiarity. The driver's door opened and a pair of tan legs appeared—then she was coming across the tarmac like it was yesterday, and Bobcat said, "Well, fuck me gently," as the girl smiled at a woman pushing a stroller and his prick began to swell in his khakis.

He left his coffee and moved to the exit, meeting the girl as she came in. He bumped shoulders with her as they passed and excused himself, giving the bill of his cap a jaunty tip. The girl gave him a dismissive glance and picked up her pace. He paused to watch her join a lineup, figuring he had maybe ten minutes if she decided to eat her grub on the fly, twenty if she dined in the restaurant.

Bobcat walked to the rear entrance of the camper and climbed inside. He'd stowed a pair of baggy Bermudas and a loud Hawaiian shirt back here and he changed into them now, stuffing the work clothes he'd been wearing into a plastic grocery bag. He traded the ballcap for a floppy beach hat and his cowboy boots for sandals, then parked the rig in a vacant spot next to the Jetta. The vehicles were about eight rows out from the restaurant—

maybe a hundred feet—which in terms of cover wasn't great, but it'd have to do. He wasn't going to lose this one again.

He switched off the ignition and let Sammy out of the carrier, the dog bounding into his lap to lick his chin. Bobcat scratched him behind the ear, knowing how much the little mutt loved it. "Atta boy, Sammy," he said. "You know what to do, right, little buddy? You know what to do." He gave the dog a Greenie, Sammy's favorite, and the girl came out of the restaurant with a paper bag in one hand and a cup of coffee in the other.

Bobcat put his shades back on, saying, "Okay, Sambo, it's show time." He got a grip on the dog's leather collar and unlatched the van door, feeling the dog tense under his hand, telling him to hold on now, boy. Hold on…

* * *

Trish came out of the restaurant checking her watch, her summer dress belling in the morning breeze. She was making excellent time and probably could have eaten inside, but experience had taught her that highway travel was at best unpredictable; besides, she wanted to be there at least an hour ahead of time. She knew her dad was nervous about getting his one-year chip, and she hoped that having her there early might help him relax. Today was one of the proudest days of his life—hers, too—and she wanted to share as much of it with him as she could.

In the Jetta she secured her coffee in the cup holder and set her meal on the passenger seat, then reached for the handle to pull the door shut. As she did, a small brown-and-white terrier clambered into her lap, making her squeal in surprise and delight. In an instant the dog was licking her cheek, its stubby tail going a mile a minute. Laughing, Trish had to grab the little guy's collar and rake her head back to keep him from lathering her entire face in dog slobber.

She said, "Hey, little fella, where'd you come from?"

Now a shadow fell across her, and Trish looked up into the grinning mug of the guy she assumed owned the dog. He was dressed like a reject from a Hawaiian Punch commercial and had a dirty old dog leash in his hand. She couldn't see his eyes through his sunglasses, but she could feel them slithering on her skin.

The dog scrambled off her lap onto the passenger seat now, its busy nose probing her breakfast bag.

The guy said, "Is that little peckerwood botherin' you, ma'am?" and the hackles bristled on her neck. She slotted the key in the ignition and turned it, thanking God the engine started on the first try. The guy was leaning on the roof of the car now and Trish saw him make a quick scan of the parking lot.

"Your pup's pretty cute," she said, "but I do have to be on my way."

He said, "Course you do," and leaned into the car, saying, "Come on outa there now, Sammy. Pay attention to your daddy." He smelled of stale sweat and rotten breath and Trish wanted him out of her face.

Tail wagging, the dog barked but made no move to obey, and when Trish reached for him he leaped into the

Last Call

back seat, toenails skidding on the body of the guitar. She leaned after him and heard the guy say, "Mutt thinks I'm fuckin' around," and felt something graze the back of her head as she moved. With a surprised yelp Trish twisted in her seat and saw a black leather object in the guy's hand, some kind of club, the guy raising it now for another attack, and she got her hands up into his face, dislodging his glasses and going for his eyes.

Then he had her by the throat, forcing her down across the seats, and he punched her hard in the face, two quick jabs that dazed her, the dog barking frenziedly now in counterpoint to Trish's strangled screams. She thought, *Why doesn't somebody come?* and her clawing fingers snagged his necklace, breaking it, sending those small white carvings flying everywhere. She thought, *Good*, and, *Get that dog off my dad's guitar...*

Now he was coming at her with that black thing again—it looked like a flat leather spoon—and he swatted her on the forehead with it and the world went gray, her last perception the barking of that little dog, echoing then receding down a long dark shaft.

* * *

Bobcat said, "Sammy, shut your hole," and the dog hunkered down with its muzzle on its paws, averting its eyes. Still straddling the unconscious girl, Bobcat popped his head up to scan the parking lot, ready to fight any heroes if he had to. But everything was business as usual out there, a dozen or so dull-eyed automatons milling around with their phones out, oblivious.

He ran a hand across his neck where she'd clawed him and it came away bloody. He said, "Bitchcat," and started picking up the carvings from his necklace. The goddam things were everywhere: in the footwells, between the seats, *under* the seats, in the door compartments, he even found one in the girl's coffee cup when he emptied it onto the floor mat. He got as many as he could, then backed out of the car to scope the parking lot again.

A few rows over a young couple glanced his way as they strolled toward the restaurant. Bobcat waited until they were inside, then lifted the girl into the passenger seat of the camper and closed the door behind her. He strolled around to the driver's side and climbed aboard, then leaned across the girl's limp body and opened the window. He said, "Sambo, up," and the dog leaped across the gap into the camper. Scratching the dog's ear, Bobcat said, "Good boy, Sammy," and gave him another treat.

He got the camper rolling and entered the feeder lane. On the highway he pulled the girl's head into his lap and poked a finger into her mouth, running it over her lovely teeth.

No damage.

"Good," he said. "Okay, good." He told Sammy to get back in the carrier, then settled into the right-hand lane, doing the speed limit.

* * *

Last Call

A few minutes later an O.P.P. cruiser pulled into a vacant spot behind the Jetta and the driver climbed out. She'd missed breakfast this morning and was looking forward to a toasted English muffin and a large double-double. On her way past the Jetta she noticed the open door, the running engine and the vintage guitar in the back seat and thought it odd. Then she saw the spatters of fresh blood on the seats and called it in, instinct telling her that something very bad had just taken place here. Seeing the red ribbon on that guitar, she cursed under her breath, wishing she'd arrived just a few minutes earlier.

11

IN THE BASEMENT of Apostles Anglican Church in North York, a small group of people sat in rows of folding chairs, chatting and sipping coffee. A few others milled about the spacious room, laughing and catching up with friends. At the big chrome coffee urn by the entrance, attendees filled paper cups with steaming brew, spooning in generous heaps of Coffee-Mate. The overall mood was festive—it was a speaker meeting this morning, celebrating a solid member's first full year of sobriety—but there was a spreading air of impatience now, too, the 10:30 meeting still not underway. The digital clock above the entrance read 10:46.

At the front of the room Jim Gamble stood by the podium with the meeting's chairman, a rotund ex-biker named Sid. Jim had put on some weight over the past several months, most of it muscle, and his tremor had all but vanished. He was boxing again, paying for lessons—and groceries and rent—out of a regular paycheck from the job he'd acquired four months ago, ironically, working the pot sinks in the cafeteria at the Toronto General Hospital. He was healthier than he'd ever been in his adult life, clear-eyed and alert, and he was proud of that.

Checking the time, Sid said, "Jesus, Jimmy boy, we got to get underway here. Nothing more vicious than a room full of juice heads kept waiting."

Jim scanned the room again, hoping to see Trish's smiling face, but there was still no sign of her. He looked at Dean seated front-and-center with his cell phone to his ear and saw him shake his head.

Jim said, "Okay, chum. Might as well get started."

Sid banged the gavel on the podium and the stragglers started filing to their seats.

* * *

During the ten-minute preamble, Jim stood with Dean at the back of the room, Dean trying Trish's number every few minutes and getting only voice mail. Jim was genuinely worried now, picturing her car breaking down or worse, an accident out there on the highway. It wasn't like her not to call if she was running late.

Jim was watching Dean dial her number again when he heard Sid call his name, and when he turned he saw everyone in the room craning their necks to look at him.

Sid said, "You're up, man."

* * *

Dean stowed his cell phone and followed Jim to the podium. He was worried now, too; but this was Jim's day and, common things being common, Trish had probably just had some car trouble en route and was marooned somewhere outside of cell range. There were long stretches of dead air all along that highway, especially further north, and chances were good she was stuck in one of them. He thought of calling her home number—the other possibility was that she'd hit the snooze button on her alarm and was still sound asleep—but if her mother picked up, he didn't want to have to explain why he was calling the house.

Now Sid left the podium and Dean stepped up, adjusting the mic to his height, saying, "Good morning, everyone, my name is Dean and I'm an addict and an alcoholic."

There was a chorused, "Hi, Dean."

Smiling, he turned to Jim, the man in constant, nervous motion now, and said, "Jim, I just want to tell you how proud I am to have been your sponsor during this difficult year. Your journey is a powerful demonstration of a fundamental principle of recovery. And that is that if you truly embrace the program, as you have, if you live it each day with faith, honesty and integrity, good things will always come from bad."

He retrieved the medallion from his shirt pocket and slipped it out of its glassine envelope. Handing it to Jim, he said, "I'm honored to present you with this chip celebrating one full year of sobriety. What you've accomplished is nothing short of a miracle, and on behalf of everyone here I'd like to wish you many more years of the same." He took Jim's hand and shook it. "Congratulations, my friend. You're an inspiration to us all."

There was a hearty round of applause. As he left the podium Dean scanned the room again, but there was still no sign of Trish.

* * *

She came to with a terrible headache, groggy and disoriented. She couldn't move, and realized only gradually that she was strapped to a chair of some kind, her head raked back so far all she could see was the water-stained ceiling. In those initial moments of disorientation, she thought she must be dreaming—then that little dog was in her lap again, and she remembered the attack, and panic surged through her like a raw amphetamine. She tried to cry out but produced only a wet, inarticulate gurgle, and realized that her mouth had been propped open somehow. She could feel cold metal rods against her tongue and palate now, and something like blunt claws or hooks stretching the corners of her mouth. She had a bad moment when she thought she might drown in the pool of saliva that had accumulated at the back of her throat, but after a few tries she managed to swallow it.

Then he was beside her, shooing the dog off her lap, leaning over to look in her mouth, the stink of him making her want to vomit.

Giving her that peaches 'n' cream grin, he said, "God *damn*, girl, these ivories are *flaw*less. Not one filling. Jesus in a jacked-up sidecar, you are the *one*." He aimed a penlight into her mouth. "And lookit this. A *di*amond. My, aren't we the trendy little cooze."

Helpless tears flooded Trish's eyes. She knew he was going to kill her—this had to be the guy who'd abducted those other girls—and she thought about never seeing her mom again, or Stacey or Dean, and in that moment she made a fierce, little girl's wish that her dad would come and save her.

Now he showed her a syringe filled with amber fluid, saying, "Normally I'd keep you nice and alert for your surgery."

Surgery?

"But today I'm gonna cut you some slack. We don't wanna risk chipping these beauties, now do we."

Trish felt the jab of a needle in her arm, then a spreading bloom of warmth in her face and chest.

"You fucked up my favorite necklace and you gouged my neck pretty good, and for that I oughta feed you to the Rotties…"

She tried to concentrate, tried to gauge his intentions from his words, but his voice was breaking apart like a weak radio signal now, and she was sinking again, down into that bottomless black shaft.

* * *

Jim examined the medallion as the applause subsided and Dean returned to his seat. It was an oval-shaped disc with some heft to it, the A.A. logo in red on the front and an inscription on the back that read, *Jim G, 1 year. Faith, Truth and Love. Serenity Group.* He squeezed it in his fist, proud for the first time in decades.

When the audience settled, Jim looked out at them and felt a swoon of terror. He'd never spoken in front of a crowd before and he wanted a drink. Wanted it bad. He rubbed his parched lips and a clown in the back row said, "Thirsty, Jim?" and everyone laughed and he was okay again. He said, "Good morning, folks, my name is Jim and I'm an alcoholic."

"Hi, Jim."

"I had my first drink when I was twelve. I was a blackout drunk from day one and there are long stretches of my life I can't even remember."

The clown said, "Probably better that way," and instead of laughter this time there were murmurs of assent.

"A guy at a speaker meeting I attended in my first week of treatment said, 'I knew I was an alcoholic when I sunburned the roof of my mouth,' and I remember thinking that was pretty funny. But tragic, too. In my years on the street I did much more damage than that, and not only to myself. So much pain. So much wasted time. But you know what? I don't regret a minute of it. Because it brought me here to all of you.

"On this very special day, I have only one regret. And that is that my daughter Trish couldn't be here to share it with me. I don't know why she didn't make it and that scares me. Caring is new to me and it can be pretty terrifying. I'm sure she's fine…but I'm afraid. I wanted to tell her…"

Tears scalded Jim's eyes and he cuffed them away.

"I wanted to tell her in front of everyone here how grateful I am that she brought me into her life. The first

Last Call

time she laid eyes on me I was fresh out of the gutter, more dead than alive in a hospital bed. She told me once how she used to imagine I'd be someone special, a heart surgeon or an executive, something like that. When she saw me that day in the hospital, she could've just walked away and I'd've been none the wiser. But she didn't." He looked at the vacant doorway, still wishing she'd whisk through it red-faced, out of breath and apologetic, but here and safe.

The tears got away on him now and he let them.

"I wanted to thank you for that, Trish, and tell you that...you make me feel like I'm someone special."

He looked again at the crowd; there wasn't a dry eye in the place. He said, "Thanks to you guys, I'm a citizen now. I have a social insurance number, a driver's license and a paying job. I even have a cell phone." He dug it out of his pocket and held it up, sending a tinkle of laughter through the room. "Although I barely know how to use the damned thing. It's a flip phone, which I think is cool as hell, but my daughter and Dean here keep ragging me about it. It's a new age when something as amazing as this little sucker can be out of fashion in under a year." He put the phone away and held up the medallion. "Thank you for this, and for what it represents. Like Dean said, for me, this is a miracle. I'll treasure it always."

Jim left the podium and moved down the center aisle, shaking the hands that were offered and flinching at the hearty back-claps he received along the way. A fearful apprehension had taken root in his heart, and with each step he took toward that empty doorway it shaped itself more vividly into a terrible certainty.

Something bad had happened to his daughter.

And it was his fault.

* * *

Trish stood naked before Bobcat, the sick bastard lounging in his torture chair like a Lord, sipping beer and petting that evil little dog in his lap. Her mouth was a throbbing, bloody wound, the tip of her tongue probing each raw socket as if by its own volition. She had her arms crossed over her breasts, all she could manage to deflect his greasy gaze.

He set the dog on the floor now, saying, "Lower them arms, girl. I wanna see them perky little titties."

A vicious *Fuck you* rose to Trish's lips and she choked it off, her mother's voice in her head now, telling her to do whatever the man said, whatever would keep her alive. *Then the first chance you get, kick him in the balls and run like hell.*

She lowered her arms.

He said, "That's better," and undid his belt. "Now, how about you do a nice little dance for Bobby. We're gonna have us a talent show tonight," he said, looking past Trish to the redheaded woman on the floor behind her; naked, gagged and bound, she'd clearly spent some time with Bobcat already. "The winner gets to live."

Trish began to dance.

***

Dean said, "Why don't I make the call. Her mom's used to hearing from me."

They were in Jim's room now, in the halfway house he shared with a group of recovering alcoholics.

Shaking his head, Jim said, "I'm done hiding, kid," and opened his cell phone. "If Trish picks up, no harm done, she can tell her mom about me in her own good time. But if something's happened to her, then I'm responsible."

He sat on a chair and dialed the number.

***

Sally grabbed the phone on the first ring. She was a basket case. Trish had promised to call as soon as she got to the flower shop, which should have been no later than ten this morning. It was after seven P.M. now, and neither she nor Sadie had heard a word from her. And the mailbox on her cell phone was full.

She said, "Hello?" There was a beat of silence and she said, "Trish, is that you?"

"No, Sally, it's Jim. Jim Gamble."

"Is this some kind of joke?"

"It's no joke. I—"

"Because whatever it is, I don't have time for it right now. I'm waiting for a call from my daughter."

***

Jim shook his head at Dean. He could hear the dread in Sally's voice, quivering just beneath the hostility, and his first instinct was to run from it, like he always had. His hand itched to break the connection.

But he said, "She's the reason I'm calling."

"What?"

"I…know her, Sally. I've known her for the past year."

"What are you talking about?"

He told her.

* * *

Bobcat tied Trish's left arm to a jack post in the center of the room. Then he lashed the redhead to the post with her back against it, extending her arms over her head, binding her legs at the ankles and thighs, stretching her pale body out as far it would go.

Now he pulled Trish into position behind the woman with the post between them, Trish's chest against the woman's back. Then he stood in front of the woman with a jackknife in his hand, a wicked looking thing with a hooked blade.

Grinning at Trish, he said, "I like you, little toad. You got heart. Not like this sack of meat." He slapped the woman across the face, the poor thing so numb with pain and exhaustion she was barely conscious now.

In spite of her terror, Trish wanted to kill this bastard.

Wait for your chance, honey.

He said, "So here's the deal. I'm gonna do a little …thing here. It's a bit rude, but hey, it's my party."

Trish saw him lower the knife to the woman's belly with the curved edge facing up. The woman was tiny, and Trish watched over her shoulder as the tip of the blade broke the skin below her navel, raising a bead of blood. With a low grunt he rocked the knife in and up, creating a neat incision about an inch long—Trish could actually hear the blade *pop* through the abdominal wall, like a thumb poking through a cellophane wrapper. The woman moaned but barely flinched. There was no fight left in her.

Now he withdrew the blade and held the knife out to Trish, saying, "Go ahead. Take it."

Fearful of a trick, Trish reached for the knife with her free hand—and in the last instant he snatched it away. "Don't go gettin' any ideas, now," he said, an amused lilt in his voice, like they were old pals horsing around. "You wouldn't be the first try to pigstick ol' Bobcat with that thing. My daddy gave me that knife, the cocksucker, so be careful with it."

He handed it to her again and Trish took it. Sweat had begun to bead on his forehead and upper lip, and he was puffing like a steam engine now. He seized Trish's knife hand and held the blade to the woman's neck, the tip indenting the skin. Then he dropped his pants and Trish saw his erection.

He said, "Now when I tell you, you're going to cut this toad's throat. Then it'll be over for her. Screw it up and

I'll show her hell. I'll spend the night with her and you'll get to watch. You follow?"

Trish nodded, tightening her grip on the jackknife.

The woman whispered, *"Kill me."*

Then Bobcat looked down at himself and Trish swung the knife, aiming for the prominent blood vessels in the man's neck. In the last possible instant he flinched away and the blade missed its target, plunging instead into the meat of his shoulder. Bobcat shrieked and punched Trish in the face, the knife springing from her hand. He pulled up his pants, then bent to retrieve the weapon, saying, "Alright, that *fucks* the mood."

He grabbed Trish's bound wrist, pinned her hand to the jack post and chopped off her baby finger. Trish screamed and the world went dark again.

* * *

Jim sat hunched in his chair, spent and ashamed. He'd told Sally all of it, and now there was only silence. From the nearby couch, Dean looked on.

Now Sally said, "I'm not surprised she found you. She just wouldn't let it go. As soon as she could talk she started asking about you. But I always put her off."

Jim said, "I don't blame you."

"She's never lied to me before. Not about anything this big. I suppose I brought it on myself." There was a pause and Sally said, "I'm not sure how I feel about this yet, Jim, okay? And I can't deal with it right now. I'm very worried about her."

Jim could hear her crying now.

Sally said, "She's headstrong, Gamble, but she's got a tender heart. If you hurt her…"

"I hear you, Sal. All I can tell you is that life is different for me now. I respect Trish, and…I love her."

"Look, I'd better get off."

"Will you call me if you hear anything?"

"Yeah," Sally said. "Alright. What's your number?"

* * *

Sally scribbled Jim's number on a pad and hung up the phone, a part of her impressed that he'd managed to surface from so low, but a greater part already blaming him for whatever was going on with Trish. In the old days everything the man touched had turned to shit, and she saw no reason to expect any different from him now.

She was dialing Trish's number again when the door bell rang.

She opened the door on two police officers and felt her heart plummet in her chest. She leaned against the doorjamb to keep herself from falling and said, "Yes?"

The older cop said, "Is this the residence of Trisha West?"

Please, God, let my baby be okay. "Yes."

"Is she the registered owner of a brown, two-thousand-five Volkswagen Jetta?"

"Yes, she is. Has there been an accident?"

The younger cop said, "Ma'am, may we come inside?"

Sick with dread, Sally let them in.

* * *

When Trish regained consciousness she was strapped to the barber chair again, facing the room, and she saw Bobcat cutting the woman down, the man cursing and raving now, blood oozing from the knife wound in his shoulder. She glanced at the aching stump of her baby finger and saw that he'd cauterized it somehow, the blunt end charred black. At least it wasn't bleeding.

The woman had passed out, and when he freed her wrists she collapsed in a boneless heap. Dropping to one knee, Bobcat jerked her head up and scowled at Trish.

"Get ready for some real entertainment, smartass," he said. "And while you're watching, remember, this is on your head."

He ran the blade along the woman's hairline, as if to scalp her, and her eyes popped open blue and wide in her bloody face and she screamed. Sick to her stomach, Trish closed her eyes and heard him say, "I see you shut them eyes again or try to look away, I'll blind you. Now pay attention."

Trish opened her eyes and watched, praying to God this would all end soon.

Daddy, please come get me...please hurry...

* * *

Jim answered the phone on the first ring. It was Sally.

Last Call

"This is *your* fault, you son of a bitch. Why couldn't you just leave well enough alone?"

"Sally, what—?"

"They found her car…it was still running and there was blood on the seat. She's *gone*, Gamble. My sweet baby girl is gone…"

* * *

Later that evening a detective by the name of Dan Boland came to the halfway house and sat with Jim and Dean on the porch. The house was situated in a quiet neighborhood in downtown Toronto, and tonight a cool breeze was blowing. The ember on Boland's cigar stitched through the dark as he raised it to his mouth, then lowered it to tell them what he thought.

"There was a series of similar disappearances last summer," Boland said.

Dean said, "I remember."

"Seven young women that we know of, all on or near the highway."

Jim said, "Have any of them been found?"

"Not yet, but all seven cases are still active. When the disappearances ended last fall we assumed the guy had either relocated or retired, but there've been three new reports already this spring, and your daughter's circumstances certainly fit the pattern. Who knows what triggers a guy like this: the moon, the seasons. The blood in your daughter's car is the first evidence of a struggle we've seen, indicating that maybe the other disappearances weren't simply voluntary, people for whatever reason deciding to leave their normal lives behind, jump on a plane to the South Seas, maybe, or open a restaurant in Australia. I've seen it happen before." The detective took a drag on his cigar, letting the smoke waft out as he said, "We're hoping some of the blood is his."

"Assuming that's what happened to her," Dean said.

"Exactly," Boland said. "That's our operative assumption. We should have the Jetta stripped down by tomorrow afternoon. Jim, if you can come by the station and have a look at whatever turns up, that would be extremely helpful. Outside of that, it's pretty much a wait-and-see proposition. Nothing tougher I can think of, but..."

Boland shrugged and stood. Jim and Dean shook hands with the man and Jim said, "I'll see you tomorrow, then." They watched the detective return to his car, then went back inside.

Jim had left a pot of coffee simmering on a hot plate, and now they sat across from each other at the breakfast nook in the kitchenette, sipping the strong blend. There was a radio on in another room, tuned to a heavy metal station, and the muted thump of the bass track seemed to pace Jim's frantic heartbeat. His nerve endings were sizzling like butter on a skillet, his sober mind serving up one horrific image after another—Trish in the hands of a psychopath somewhere—and the helplessness he felt was making him so damned *thirsty*—

Dean said, "She's wrong, you know."

"What?"

"Trish's mom. She's wrong. Whatever's happened, wherever Trish is, it's not your fault."

Jim felt something tilt in his mind and now he was up on his feet, pelting his coffee mug against the wall, saying, "She's fucking-A *right* is what she is. I never should've let Trish drive down here so early. Aw, shit, I never should've had anything to do with her in the first place. All my life I've found a way to *fuck* up everything I care about."

Dean said, "Feeling sorry for yourself isn't going to help anybody," and Jim hauled him out his seat and slammed him against the wall, saying, "Pissant. What do you know about it?"

Dean seized Jim's thumb and cranked it hard, then bent him over and put him in a headlock, immobilizing him. Now he pressed his forehead to Jim's temple and said in his ear, "I know I love her just as much as you do. I know she'd love *you* if you were stroked out and shitting your diaper in a wheelchair. And I know your risk of relapse right now is sky high. I don't want to see that happen and I know Trish wouldn't either."

Dean let him go, shoving him away, and Jim whirled to face him. There was a tense moment, an old and still-sick part of Jim wanting to duke it out…then he shook his head and slumped back into his seat. He wiggled his thumb and winced. "Shit, kid, that was pretty good. Where'd you learn to do that?"

"I bounced a couple summers at a strip joint," Dean said, sitting now, too.

Jim gazed out the window to the street, nothing moving out there. He said, "What are we going to do?"

Dean had no answer.

* * *

Bobcat shoved her backward into the hole. Trish spun as she fell, managing to land on her feet on the mucky bottom, but her momentum pitched her hard against the dirt wall, the sharp stump of a root gouging her shoulder, and when she touched it her fingers came away bloody. She looked up and saw him leering down at her over the rim of the pit.

"Hope you're satisfied," he said. "Now I gotta find us a new toy."

He was dragging a big metal plate over the opening now, the veins in his forearms bulging with the strain, and Trish felt oddly relieved, thinking she'd rather be alone down here, cold and naked in a hole in the ground, than anywhere near that murdering bastard.

Still holding the metal plate, he leaned over the hole to say, "You're gonna learn to do what I tell you—" and the jackknife slipped out of his shirt pocket and tumbled into the pit. Trish caught it in mid air—and his whole demeanor changed, a bitter petulance coming into his voice now, Bobcat saying, "You throw that back up here now, girl. I am not fucking with you on this subject." He dropped the metal plate, then lay on the ground and thrust his arm down at her, spreading his fingers to catch the knife. "Toss it up."

Trish opened the blade. "Why don't you come down here and get it?"

"Alright," he said, standing. "Wanna play? Alright. You go ahead and hold onto it for me. It's not like you're going anywhere."

He covered the hole with the plate, and Trish was fearful now that the price of her small victory might be her life. She shouldn't have provoked him. She imagined him going back to the house for a gun or flooding the hole with a garden hose, and she raised her voice to say, "Are you still there? I was just kidding, okay? Come back and I'll give you the knife, I promise."

She waited but he didn't respond. At least he'd left the light on up there, thin rays of it reaching her through the air holes in the plate.

It occurred to her to try climbing to the top, but the walls sloped inward as they rose, the crumbly surface offering few handholds, only the occasional flimsy root or half-buried rock. And even if she made it all the way up, there'd be no way she could move that metal slab.

She closed the knife and sat on a narrow dirt platform that was drier than the flooded bottom. Now that he was gone, she was glad to have the knife and would try to use it on him again if he came back.

Trish studied her surroundings in the meager light, seeing the shallow tunnel someone had dug in a vain attempt at escape, seeing fecal matter floating in the ground water and a tuft of blonde hair snagged on the splintered end of a root partway up the wall. She noticed a trickle of water seeping in through a channel in the wall above her head and opened the knife again, wedging the blade into the channel now. A few seconds later the trickle found its way into the groove in the handle, then drizzled off the butt end into thin air, the water mucky at first, then running clear. Trish opened her mouth and let the cool liquid soothe her parched lips and tongue.

Shivering now, Trish wrapped her arms around her legs and pulled them tight to her chest, trying to keep warm. Her mouth throbbed with pain and her gummy saliva tasted like copper. She was more terrified than she'd ever been.

A few minutes later she heard him come back into the barn and turn off the light, pitching her prison into the most seamless dark she'd ever experienced.

Faintly she heard him say, "Sleep well, little toad."

Then there was nothing, save the distant chirr of crickets.

* * *

Bobcat stalked out of the barn saying, "Let you age down there a while, then feed you to the Rotties." Nervy toad, stealing his knife like that. Where'd she think she was going with it, anyways? That knife was the only thing his daddy ever gave him, besides a beating, and as much as he hated the mean bastard, he cherished that knife very much. Every time he held it he remembered how easily it had opened the old man's throat. If she broke that thing he'd make her eat her own kidneys. *Fuck me.* A perfect finish to a fucked up day.

He slammed the door coming into the house and Sammy yipped and spun to look at him. The little mutt had been sniffing the mess on the floor and Bobcat told him to get the fuck away from there. Sammy scooted over to his basket and curled up with his back to the room, and Bobcat blinked at the woman's raw, tangled corpse, feeling a momentary confusion, as if seeing it for the first time. Really *seeing* it.

When he was a boy his ma used to tell him he needed to find some friends his own age and stop killing things, and sometimes he wished he'd listened. Bringing in stock for the work was one thing, but Jesus, didn't he maybe take it too far sometimes? He couldn't be sure. All he knew for certain was that it was a goddam messy business.

He said, "Gotta clean this shithole up, Sammy," and the dog stood to face him in its basket, that stubby tail starting up. "Gotta clean this fucker up."

He went into the workshop and came back with a chainsaw, a handful of heavy-duty garbage bags and a yellow hardhat with a plastic visor. He put on the hardhat, visor up, and grabbed the dead woman's ankles.

She left a slippery snail trail across the floor and down the porch steps and Bobcat said, "Fucking mess, will it ever end?" some vestige of humanity making him cringe at the sound of her head thumping each wooden tread. He dragged her into the dooryard and tossed the garbage bags on the ground, watching them fan out like a blank poker hand. Then he pulled down the visor and started the chainsaw.

As he bent to his work, the sun breeched the horizon behind him.

12

Tuesday, June 28

JIM SAT ALONE at a round table in a police interrogation room, clutching a cup of coffee from the vending machine in the lobby. The brew was pretty bad, bitter and strong, but he hadn't slept a wink and now he was grateful for the mild caffeine buzz.

Startling him, Detective Boland came in with Sally in tow and Jim got to his feet, surprised and a little shocked to see her again after so many years, wishing now that it were under less trying circumstances. Boland hadn't told him she was coming, but Jim knew the way a cop's mind worked, always assuming guilt, looking for ways to trip people up. At first blush it diminished his opinion of the man, but then he realized the detective was only doing his job in the best way he knew how. Of course the parents would be suspects in a case like this, and of course a good cop would bring stress to the interrogation in whichever way he could. And Jim wasn't kidding himself; whatever else Boland might be calling this little get together, it was an interrogation.

Though Sally looked shattered, she was still just as beautiful as he remembered her, and as she approached the table he held out his hand to her. Scowling, Sally said,

"Don't—touch me," and Jim returned to his chair, stung, averting his gaze as she took a seat across from him. Boland offered her coffee and Sally said, "Can we just get this done?"

Boland said of course and set a small cardboard box on the table between them. Looking at Jim, he said, "These are the items that were found in your daughter's—" and Sally said, "She's *my* daughter, Detective Boland."

"I apologize, Ms. West," Boland said. "These are the things we found in your daughter's car. We need to know what belongs to Trish and what—if anything—doesn't. Anything you've never seen before could be evidence."

He removed a stack of clear plastic baggies from the box, each of them sealed and affixed with a red evidence sticker. He handed the top one to Sally, who examined it—a pack of Juicy Fruit gum—and said, "I can't be certain this exact one is hers, but it is her favorite flavor." Nodding, Boland took it back and handed it to Jim, who concurred. Then he gave Sally the second bag and replaced the first one in the box.

They proceeded in this fashion until Sally said, "I've never seen this before," and handed the bag back to Boland. The detective read the evidence sticker, saying, "It's a piece of handmade jewelry, from a charm bracelet, probably, or a necklace. It was wedged down in the seat mechanism." He handed it to Jim now, saying, "It got broken trying to free it up."

Jim squinted at the two small but elaborate fragments, a carving of an animal of some kind, a cat maybe, or a squirrel. Some of the detail was missing along the edges of the break, which ran almost straight through the center of the item, but Jim could see that it was a fine piece of craftsmanship. It looked like it was made of ivory or maybe bone.

Boland said, "Could it belong to your daughter?"

"I'd have to say yes," Sally said. "She loves stuff like that. She's got a ton of it at home."

Boland said, "One of our investigators will have to go through all of that," and Sally said, "Of course."

Jim said, "Can I take this thing out?"

Boland said, "Sure," and took the bag from him, breaking the seal and handing him the contents. "Do you recognize it?"

Jim said, "No, I've never seen it before. There's just something…" He rubbed one of the broken halves between his fingertips, feeling the slightly oily texture of the fractured surface. It put him in mind of something, but he couldn't narrow it down. After a moment he shook his head and handed the fragments back to the detective. "I guess it's nothing," he said. "It just seemed to ring a bell for a second there."

"That's alright," Boland said, replacing the objects in the bag. "The car had three previous owners and we'll be checking in with each of them as well. But if anything comes to you later on, either of you, please be sure to give me a call. In a case like this, every detail is important."

They went through the last few bags without further query, either Jim, Sally or both able to verify that the items belonged to Trish.

When they were done, Boland said, "With your permission, we'd like to draw blood samples from you both before you leave. As you know, there was blood in the car; the DNA studies will help us determine if it was your daughter's."

Jim thought, *And exclude us as suspects.*

Sally said, "Those other girls, Detective, the ones that disappeared. Do you think the same thing's happened to my daughter? Do you think someone got her?"

Boland said, "It's too early to say for certain, Ms. West. The staff at the restaurant don't recall serving her, but hundreds of people go through that place every hour. We've subpoenaed their security footage and should have it in hand by the end of the day. Maybe we'll find something there. Another possibility is the car was stolen somewhere en route and your daughter was never even at the restaurant."

Jim almost told him the restaurant was her usual food stop en route from Sudbury, but decided to let him know later, in private. It was clear Sally was close to the breaking point and wanted only to get out of here.

Boland said, "I do need to ask you both—and I apologize for this in advance—but is there any chance your daughter was involved with illicit drugs or with anyone in that world?"

Sally quickly denied it, but Jim said, "Dean, her boyfriend, was into that about a year-and-a-half ago—"

Sally said, "Jesus Christ."

"—but Trish broke it off with him as soon as she found out. Dean went into rehab that same week and he's been

Last Call

my sponsor in the recovery program for the past year. No way he's into that shit anymore."

Boland said, "Thank you, Jim. We've got him coming in later today, and I'm assuming he'll be forthcoming on the subject."

Jim said, "He will."

Boland said, "One last thing, then. Is there any chance Trish ran away? Any huge fight or disagreement she might have had with either of you? Any new boyfriends who might have lured her away?"

Jim said, "No way," and Sally said, "Listen, Detective Boland, I understand why you've got to ask these questions, and I appreciate you being thorough. But let me assure you right now, once and for all, that my daughter is a *good* girl. She always has been. She's bright, focused — she's on her way to becoming a veterinarian, for Christ sake — so please, this instant, put all that horseshit out of your mind and just *find* my daughter, okay? Just find my little girl…"

Jim touched Sally's arm, he couldn't help himself, and now she turned on him like a jackal, striking his face and chest with her fists, Jim making no move to protect himself, Sally shouting, "I told you not to *touch* me, you junkie asshole. *This is all your* fault!"

Boland broke it up and led Sally out of the room. Through the open door Jim saw him hand her off to a female officer, who led her away to have her blood drawn. Sick in his guts, Jim only stood there, tasting blood on his lips.

Boland came back and led him to a chair, handing him a tissue for his bloody nose, saying, "That was a bad scene. I'm sorry."

"I had it coming."

"Still."

"I'm okay," Jim said. "I'm ready to have that blood drawn now." Grinning, he held out the bloody tissue. "Unless this'll do."

Laughing, Boland said, "Sometimes all you *can* do is laugh," and started for the door. He said, "I'll have someone come get you for the blood work." Then: "Oh, before I forget. Come with me, would you?"

Jim got up and followed the detective to his third floor office, a small angular space in a corner of the building. The walls were plastered with wanted posters and crime scene photos, the desk in the corner equally cluttered with official looking documents and computer equipment.

Boland reached into a tiny closet and came out with a vintage acoustic guitar, a big red ribbon tied in a bow around the rosewood neck. Jim knew right away who it was from. She was always talking about him getting back into music, wanting to hear him play.

Boland gave him the guitar, then took a big red envelope out of a desk drawer and handed that to him, too. He said, "This came with it."

Jim leaned the guitar against the desk and opened the card, going straight to the inscription. In Trish's elegant script, it read simply, *Congratulations, Dad. I am so proud of you!!!!* It was signed, *Your daughter. xxxooo*

Heading for the door now, Boland said, "Why don't you take a few minutes, Jim. Then we'll get that blood work out of the way."

Jim nodded as Boland left. He sat in the chair in front of the desk and picked up the guitar, a beautiful old Gibson Hummingbird, and strummed the open strings. *Have to tune 'er up*, he thought, and wept more violently than he'd ever imagined possible.

13

Thursday, July 7

JIM THOUGHT, *SHIT*. Some rude bitch at the cop shop had put him on hold, an annoying disco tune thumping in his ear now. *Jesus Christ.*

He rubbed his lips with a sweaty hand, feeling like he had that first week in treatment, the alcohol still leaving his system. The shakes had returned, not full-blown but still pretty bad, and the hunger was alive in him again. He needed *some*thing. He hadn't been to an A.A. meeting in over a week, and in view of the situation, asking Dean to put on his sponsor hat right now seemed unforgivably self-centered. The poor kid was losing his mind, too.

A gruff male voice said: "Boland."

Finally. "Detective, it's Jim Gamble. Do you have any news for me?"

"Nothing yet, Jim. We—"

"Shit, man, that's not good enough. It's been ten *days*. What are you people doing out there?"

"I understand your frustration, Jim," Boland said, sounding distracted, "but believe me, we're doing everything we can."

Jim said, "Yeah, well I'm sick of waiting." He cut the connection and called Dean, saying, "I need your car."

"Sure," Dean said. "What's up?"

"I'm going out to look for her."

"Give me an hour. I'm coming with you."

* * *

Dean arrived forty minutes later in his Beemer. Jim climbed in with an army surplus duffel bag and sat with it on his knees. Dean took the bag and tossed it on the back seat next to a small suitcase. He said, "Where to?"

Jim showed him some photos of Trish. "I thought we could start at the restaurant. Show her picture around. It's a needle in a haystack, but I can't sit around here any longer. I'm going out of my mind."

"I hear that," Dean said. "Let's go find her."

* * *

They were silent for most of the trip, each man immersed in his own dark musings. When they got to the restaurant Jim asked to see the manager, who turned out to be a decent guy with three daughters of his own. He led them to his office, a cramped, windowless space in the back next to the staff washroom, and had the employees file through one at a time to look at Trish's picture. As it turned out, the majority of them hadn't even been working that day, and the ones who were didn't recall serving her. Everyone was polite and sympathetic, but like Jim had said at the outset, it was a needle in a haystack. They thanked the manager and gratefully accepted

Last Call

the free burgers, drinks and fries he offered to help them on their way.

They went to the gas bar next and Dean topped up the tank while Jim canvassed the staff; but again, no luck. They spent the next several hours checking every public place they could find—strip malls, convenience stores, gas stations—then had dinner at a greasy spoon and grabbed a few winks in the car behind a motel. The proprietor ran them off just before dawn, making a show of recording Dean's license plate number and threatening to call the cops if he ever laid eyes on them again.

***

Shortly after sun-up that morning, sixteen-year-old Jason Hanson said to his buddy Mike Zufelt, "Nice play, ass cramp. We're lost." Mike had veered off the woodlands trail about five klicks back, saying it was a short cut, and like an idiot Jason had followed. They were crawling along through dense underbrush now, the dirt bikes wanting to stall at such low speeds, and Jason was about to say screw it and double back when he spotted something odd in a nearby clearing.

He said, "Hey, man, check this out," and accelerated into the clearing, seeing a bunch of green garbage bags hanging like ponderous fruit from the low branches of random trees around the thirty foot perimeter. The bags each looked about half full, and heavy, their contents creating smooth humps and sharp bulges in the plastic, stretching it close to the tearing point. And the whole area smelled bad, like rotten eggs.

Mike rolled up beside him now, saying, "What the hell is this?"

Jason walked his bike to the nearest bag and sliced it open with a pocket knife. Something fleshy and foul smelling slopped out and landed by his sneaker. He said, "Holy *shit*," and did a quick scan of the area, trying to look everywhere at once. Then he toed his bike into gear and gunned the engine, almost losing control, debris from the forest floor spraying Mike in the face and chest. Jason took off at full throttle, screaming like a little girl.

Certain he was being fucked with, Mike scooted over for a closer look. Then he beat it the hell out of there, too, glancing back every few seconds to make sure that whoever had strung up those bags wasn't following them.

* * *

Dean said, "You sure you're okay with this?"

They were parked outside of Zak's Roadhouse. The place was open but the gravel lot was almost abandoned, just a couple of pickups, a black SUV and an idling semi, the driver at the wheel combing his sparse hair in the rearview.

Jim said, "It's ten-thirty in the morning. I'm not thinking about booze right now, okay? I'm good."

Dean said okay and they went inside, seeing an old guy in coveralls sweeping the plank floor, a waitress swabbing tables and a massively obese bartender toweling beer mugs. Dean headed for the waitress and Jim took the barkeep, showing him Trish's picture, asking if he'd ever seen her before.

"Nope, never seen her. Who is she?"

"My daughter," Jim said. "She's missing."

The bartender had another look at the photo. "Oh, right, I seen it on the news the other night. The cops think somebody grabbed her?"

"They don't know yet."

"We had a gal grabbed right out here in the parking lot last summer. You must've heard about that? Found her next morning in a payloader, chopped in twenty pieces, not a tooth left in her... Oh, Jesus Christ, man, I'm sorry. That was in poor taste." He plunked a frosted mug on the polished bar. "Here, let me buy you a cold one."

Jim's dry tongue ran his lips and he eyed the shiny spigots. A golden drop of brew hung from the nearest one, catching the sunlight.

He said, "No thanks," and the barkeep said, "That's cool," as Jim double-timed it to the exit. "Good luck with your kid."

Dean caught up to him in the parking lot and put a hand on his shoulder, making him flinch, Dean saying, "Hey, buddy, you okay?"

Jim said, "I'm fine." But he wasn't.

"Alright, then. Let's hit the road."

Jim followed Dean back to the car, seeing that golden bead clinging to the spigot, healing elixir gleaming in the sunlight.

* * *

They spent the balance of that day engaged in an increasingly pointless pursuit, circling back over the same ground, beating it flat.

It was full dark now and Dean was nodding at the wheel, the unspooling center line lulling him perilously close to sleep. Jim drowsed beside him, muttering from some barren dreamscape.

Yawning, Dean said, "Jim?" and Jim opened his eyes. "Sorry to wake you, man, but I'm trashed. I think we should find a room for the night, okay? My treat. I can't spend another night trying to sleep in this car."

Jim agreed, turning the radio up now to catch a newsbreak: *"A grisly development in the ongoing missing persons cases,"* the newscaster said. *"A number of decayed body parts were discovered this morning in the Muskoka area woods by two local teens. So far police have declined to comment, but an informed source at the coroner's office told an Action News reporter that the remains, strung up in trees like macabre ornaments, are believed to belong to a number of young women who've gone missing in the region over the past several months."*

Jim said, "Oh, no..."

Dean silenced the radio. "Doesn't mean it's Trish," he said. "Let's get off the highway, give Boland a call."

Jim turned the radio back on.

"O.P.P. Corporal Skip Sullivan says that police specialists have many hours of work ahead of them, both at the scene and

in the forensics lab, before much more can be concluded about this horrific discovery."

Dean pulled into an abandoned rest stop and shut off the engine.

Boland had given Jim his cell number and Jim dialed it now, getting out of the car as the call connected. By the fourth ring he was standing at a guard rail overlooking a marshy lake, a pair of loons down there roosting in the moonlight. He could sense Dean behind him.

The detective said, "Boland."

Jim said, "I just heard the news."

"Jim, Jesus, I was just about to give you a call. I wanted to get to you before you heard about it that way. Listen, man, I've got to be honest with you, it doesn't look good. I've already spoken to Sally. Her sister's with her now." Jim heard the detective take a breath. "We found some of your daughter's clothing in one of the bags, and a burnt-wood talisman Sally said you made for her years ago. And...we found one of Trish's fingers, Jim. Sally verified it. There was a band aid on it she put there herself."

Something tightened in Jim's chest. "Is she dead?"

"We can't say for certain yet. The pathologist should be able to...sort things out soon enough. I told Sally not to give up hope, but to prepare herself for the worst. I'm sorry, Jim. Now that we have some solid evidence, though, we're going after this guy full throttle, setting up a command post and getting the FBI involved—"

Jim hung up. When he turned from the guard rail with tears on his face Dean said, "What did he say?"

"Trish is dead."

* * *

Dan Boland tucked his cell phone away, then flicked his cigar into the gravel behind the abandoned warehouse he'd secured as an incident command post and tactical staging area. Situated on a remote stretch of Highway 69 north of Barrie, the hangar-like structure had once been a storage depot for Goodyear Tires, the faded logo still visible above the loading bay in the light of an old porcelain gooseneck, dozens of moths up there now, bumping their dizzy heads against the caged bulb. Local authorities had confiscated the property following a multi-million dollar drug bust the previous summer, the entire back end of the place stacked to the rafters with bales of marijuana when the SWAT team broke in. Dan was friendly with the mayor, who had graciously allowed them to convene here.

Interacting with the family members of murder victims was the part of the job Dan most dreaded—and the part he was least adept at—and after speaking to Jim Gamble he allowed himself a few minutes alone out here in the dark, sucking the clean country air into his lungs and thinking he might puke, the taste of that cigar souring his stomach.

He wanted to call the man back, do a better job of it, but he knew it was too late. Why in God's name had he started talking about the investigation? Jim had to know that what he'd meant by 'solid evidence' included his daughter's severed finger. What the man needed right now was compassion, not clinical details and bullshit bravado. Small wonder the guy hung up on him. *Fuck this case.*

A mosquito flew into Dan's ear and he slapped it too hard, setting off a bright ringing in his skull. He got the little sucker, though, a tiny smear of blood on his palm next to the insect's macerated remains.

He wiped his hand on his pants and went back inside.

The IT guys were still hard at work under the glaring fluorescents, running cables, installing computers and rigging phone lines, a few police personnel busy at the work stations already in place.

Alec Dunster, Dan's second in command, was waving him over now, the stout investigator standing in front of a large group of cops and detectives drawn from several jurisdictions, a laser pointer in his blocky hand. Tacked up on a portable display board behind him was a huge aerial map of the two hundred kilometer stretch of highway the killer had been harvesting.

Dan joined Dunster in front of the seated officers, some of their sleepy faces familiar to him, most of them not. "For those of you who don't know me," he said, "my name is Dan Boland. I'll be your case manager on this one. You've already met Detective Dunster here, the lead investigator." Dunster nodded at the crowd and Dan said, "You'll be reporting directly to him.

"To give you some idea of what we're up against here…"He removed an 8X10 glossy from a file folder and turned it face-down on the table in front of him. "The coroner estimates six different women in those garbage bags, maybe more. A chainsaw was used for the dismemberment in all cases. The coroner won't say for certain yet, but I'm betting it's the same one used in the Patty Holzer slaying last summer.

"Some of the remains were burned, others flayed, still others partially eaten by animals. The coroner figures dogs. Big ones. From variations in the bite marks, he's estimating four to six different animals. We've got somebody waking up local vets as we speak. Maybe the guy pampers these beasts: yearly check-ups, immunizations. It's worth a shot."

Dan cleared his throat. He wanted another smoke.

"IDs have been made on three of the victims so far, based on personal effects found in the garbage bags and, in the more recent case of Trisha West, confirmed tissue evidence." He held up the 8X10 glossy, a close-up of the girl's finger, the band aid still in place, the inked-on heart smeared with gore. He said, "The kid's mother put the band aid on there herself."

He tucked the photo back into the folder.

"We've asked our Behavioral Science colleagues at Quantico to compile a psychological profile on this nutcase; with any luck we'll have it in hand by tomorrow midday. We have our own people working on it, too, but with serial murder it's all about experience, and ours here in Canada—thank God—pales next to that of our neighbors to the south.

"So for the time being, ladies and gentlemen, make your presence known. And stay alert. Guys like this are addicts. They can't stop. They can leave town, set up shop elsewhere when things get too hot—and if our boy does that, we'll consider it a victory—but they cannot stop. Each time they kill and get away with it, they feel more empowered. They start believing they'll never get caught, that they're somehow invisible. And that's when they start taking chances, leaving themselves open to identification by law enforcement. Theoretically, at any rate. The sad truth is that most of these flakes, if they're apprehended at all, it's by sheer fluke. They're pulled over for a busted taillight and a sharp copper listens to his gut. Or somebody notices a bad smell coming out of the trunk of the bastard's car. Luck is a factor here, folks, so court it.

"Oh, and one last thing. He's a trophy taker. He pulls out their teeth."

Boland nodded at Dunster, his presentation complete. Returning the nod, Dunster said, "Okay, people, you have your assignments. We meet back here in twenty-four hours."

Murmuring among themselves, the task force rose en masse and headed for the exits.

***

It was after midnight when the desk clerk at the Super 8 in Barrie handed Dean a pair of room keys and wished him a pleasant stay. Dean could only nod. He felt numb, robotic, his mind unable to process the fact that Trish was gone. Just…gone. It didn't make sense, and every fiber of his being rejected it. At random intervals some pitiless scrap of hindbrain assaulted him with unbidden images of the way she must have died—single, lurid flash-frames of torture and dismemberment—but for the most part he was simply moving from one task to the next now, his conscious mind closed off to everything but the moment he was in.

Jim was standing by the lobby windows, staring into a night stained amber by sodium arc lamps. He hadn't said a word since the rest stop (*Trish is dead*) and Dean had left him to his silence.

He picked up their luggage and joined Jim at the windows, sharing his view. There was a busy commercial strip across the road—bars, casinos, topless joints—and Dean saw Jim's eyes reflected in the glass, glazed by the neon allure. He said, "We should try and get some sleep," and got no response, expecting none.

Then, as if deciding, Jim said, "You go ahead. I need some air."

"Want company?"

Jim shook his head and started for the exit. Dean went after him and gave him a key. "Room two-o-four," he said. "Be careful, Jim."

Jim said nothing and Dean returned to the windows to watch him go, the man crossing the road out there now like a zombie. A cabbie leaned on his horn and had to swerve around him, then he was on the other side, the bright lights drawing him in. Dean knew he should go after him, at least try to stop him, but he was husked out, drained of the will to do anything but lie down in the dark and pray for the refuge of sleep.

Last Call

* * *

Jim thought, *Fuck it*. For more years than he could remember, that had been his credo. Words to live by.

Fuck it.

The phrase repeated mantra-like in his mind, taking up the rhythm of his stride, forming an urgent backbeat to his inevitable surrender to a fate he'd been a fool to believe he could avoid. Trish had been his tether to a brighter world, but now that she was gone, what was the point?

His tremor had returned in earnest and the demon was wide awake now, shrieking its unappeasable need. The neon exerted a gravitational pull, and by the time he hit the sidewalk he was running.

He went into the first place he came to, Teasers, a poster on the door promising Rockin' Live Music and Rollin' Hot Babes. The place was stuffy and small, the band on break, a bored-looking waitress with pink hair strutting past him as he headed for the bar. He sat on a red leather stool next to a bearded biker and ordered a whisky neat.

The barkeep poured a glass and slid it over, spilling a drop on the bar. Jim scooped up the drop with a fingertip and brought it to his nose, his eyes rolling as the pungent aroma braced his nostrils, flooding his mouth with saliva. He shivered in anticipation of oblivion.

Jim Gamble picked up the shot glass, dumped the whisky into his mouth and threw his head back, slamming the empty onto the bar. He held that position for a long beat, as if frozen there, the cords in his neck straining against the skin...then a roar commenced deep in his chest, a sound of such consummate fury and destitution the patrons around him shrank away. As the roar escalated to a furious pitch, his mouth yawned open and the whisky appeared to boil...

He heard a sweet voice in his head then—*Dad, no*—and he lurched sideways to spew the whisky onto the floor, the bulk of it spattering the biker's boots. The biker said, "Psycho," and grabbed Jim by the collar. In the same instant Jim sprang up and slammed the biker backward over the bar, his hand closing around the man's throat, his voice drawing out like a rusty blade. "Not tonight, man. Do not fuck with me tonight."

He released the biker and backed away. A couple of bouncers appeared, but kept their distance as Jim left the bar.

* * *

Dean awoke at first light dreaming of Trish. The bed next to his hadn't been slept in and there was no sign of Jim. He dressed quickly and left the room.

He found Jim sitting on the hood of the car in lavender dawn light, sipping hot coffee. Relieved, he said, "You okay?"

Last Call

Handing him a steaming cup, Jim said, "I'm fine," and slid off the hood. "Let's go home."

14

Saturday, July 9

JIM WAS GRATEFUL that Dean was dealing with his grief in silence. During his years on the street, he'd discovered a vault deep inside himself where he'd been able to stuff his pain; and while it had been a more secure vault steeped in alcohol, it was serving him well enough now. He knew a time was coming when it would fail him and he'd have to face the unbearable truth, but he preferred to do so in isolation. For now there was only this numbness. And the hate.

They were on Highway 69 now heading north, and Dean pointed at a rustic log structure a hundred yards ahead, a portable sign on the verge identifying it as the Cold River Trading Post, one of the many places they'd canvassed on the way down. Dean said, "I've got to stop up here and use the can. My guts are a mess."

He pulled the Beemer into the busy lot and found a space between a silver Lexus and a gray campervan about fifty yards from the entrance. He pocketed the keys and told Jim he might need a while, and Jim decided to go inside. He didn't feel like talking, but he didn't want to sit out here alone, either.

The place was a typical Northern Ontario souvenir shop, stocked to the rafters with Native crafts, T-shirts, handcrafted jewelry, mineral samples and lots of sugary edibles. Patrons milled about in pairs or dragging impatient kids, trying on jackets and sunglasses, shaking their heads at the hefty price tags.

As Dean headed for the men's room, Jim approached a long display case at the front of the store, a big-bellied guy wearing a nametag that said "Hank" standing at the register, handing a wad of cash to a man in a ballcap and dark glasses. Jim saw the man pocket the cash and leave, then watched Hank stoop to add something to the display case, a small silver tray bearing an assortment of white charms that triggered a jarring cross-connection in Jim's mind. There were a bunch more of them in the lighted case.

Seeing Jim's quickening approach, Hank said, "Can I help y—?" and Jim seized one of the pieces off the tray, scattering the others to the floor. Hank said, *"Hey,"* and Jim grabbed a large geode off a display stand and sank to one knee, a creeping horror clenching his scalp. He set the carving on the plank floor and slammed the geode against it like a sledge, smashing it into three jagged pieces. Tossing the geode aside, he retrieved the largest fragment and angled it to the light of the big front window.

Hank was angry now, telling Jim he'd better pay for that thing or he'd bring the cops down on him, and Jim said, "A tooth...it's a goddamn *tooth.*"

Hank said, "What are you talking about?"

"These carvings," Jim said, rising to his full height. "Where do you get them?"

Hank aimed a sausage-size finger at him. "I remember you. You're the guy was in here the other day looking for his kid—"

"I said where do you *get* them?"

"Uh, local fella," Hank said, stumbling back a few paces. "Kinda mysterious. Comes in here couple times a month in season with a bunch of new stuff. They're very big sellers. Why did you—?"

"Do you know where he lives?"

"No idea," Hank said. He pointed at the exit. "But you just missed him."

"The guy in the sunglasses?"

Hank nodded and Jim bolted to the window.

The guy was climbing into a camper now—they'd parked right *next* to him—and Jim's first instinct was to run out there and drag the bastard out of the van. But at this distance he'd never make it; he'd only spook the guy and they'd never find him again. So he waited, watching the guy drive to the verge and signal a right-hand turn.

Then he bolted to the men's room and banged on the locked door. "Dean, get your ass out here now. It's *him*. The son of a bitch is right outside."

He heard Dean say through the door, "What? Who's outside?"

"The guy who got Trish."

Dean came out jabbing his shirttail into his pants. "How do you know?"

Trust me," Jim said, putting his hand out. "Give me the keys."

Dean gave him the keys and Jim ran flat out for the exit, Dean hot on his heels, Hank shouting, "Hey, who's going to pay for this thing?"

* * *

By the time they got to the highway the camper was just a speck on the crest of a distant hill. Jim said, *"Shit,"* and gunned it, white smoke spewing from the rear tires as they found purchase on the blacktop.

Dean said, "Can you tell me what's going on now?"

"There was something in Mandy's car, a charm of some kind, a small white carving broken in two. It looked like ivory or maybe bone, but it finally clicked in that joint back there. The guy had a bunch of them in a display case. They're made of teeth. *Human* teeth. I had a couple of my own knocked out in a bar fight once, busted into pieces in my mouth."

"What's that got to do with the guy we're chasing?"

"He's the guy who does the carvings."

Dean said, "Holy shit," and reached under the passenger seat, coming out with a sturdy plastic case. He thumbed it open on his lap and pulled out a .22 caliber pistol.

"Where'd you get that?"

"It's one of my dad's target pistols," Dean said, pointing it down the road. "Come on, man, we're losing him."

"Don't worry, I see him. I don't want him to know we're onto him. We're just—will you put that thing away?"

Dean stuffed the gun down the back of his jeans.

Jim said, "Thank you. Try not to shoot yourself in the ass." He said, "We're just going to follow him for now, see where he's holed up. Then we wait."

"For what?"

"For the fucker to fall asleep."

Dean said, "He pulls out their teeth to make *jewelry*?"

Jim nodded, his gaze fixed on the camper, a half mile ahead now.

Dean brought the gun out again and chambered a round. "This motherfucker's dead."

* * *

Twenty minutes later, the camper turned left onto an unmarked side road. Keeping his distance, Jim eased the BMW onto the shoulder and counted to ten before making the turn. The only sign of the camper now was a dense cloud of road dust, the hard-packed surface bone dry in the summer heat. The road was narrow and badly rutted, shaded by an almost uninterrupted canopy of overarching trees, and Jim had to slow to a crawl, waiting for the dust to clear.

They lost sight of the vehicle after that but kept on rolling, nowhere to go but straight ahead. Several minutes later the road forked and Jim stopped the car, no evidence in either direction now of the camper or its passing. He said, "Which way?" and Dean pointed left into a corridor of trees, no trespassing and private property signs posted every fifteen feet or so.

Jim angled left, taking his time, the tone of the signs becoming more forbidding the farther along they went: BEWARE OF DOGS, THIS PROPERTY PROTECTED BY SMITH & WESSON, TRESSPASSERS WILL BE SHOT.

Dean said, "Paranoid son of a bitch."

They crested an incline and Jim stopped the car, a rundown farmhouse appearing in the near distance, the campervan just rolling in through the arched entryway to a machinery barn in the field behind the house. With the exception of the roadway, the property was surrounded by bush, no signs of cattle or other domestic animals. This was not a working farm.

"Okay," Jim said. "Dead end. That's where he's holed up." He shifted into Reverse and turned to look out the rear window. "We'll wait back at the fork until dark—"

Dean jumped out of the car and started down the road in a commando-style crouch, the .22 aimed at the sky.

Cursing, Jim parked the car and went after him, saying, "What the hell are you doing?"

"You go back to the fork," Dean said. "I just wanna check it out." He took off again and Jim followed, Dean cutting into the woods now to the right of the road, angling through the undergrowth toward the back of the house. There were a few other outbuildings back here not visible from the road, a couple of storage sheds and what looked like an unused outhouse, the plank door hanging askew by one of the hinges. There was a big chain-link kennel with a corrugated roof about thirty feet from the back porch, penning at least six large black dogs, two of them pacing with their noses to the ground, the others drowsing in the sun. Jim thought, *Rottweilers. Fucker wasn't lying about the dogs.*

Dean reached the tree line and sank to one knee, the house a hundred yards away now across a field of hip-high cord grass and wildflowers.

Coming up behind him, Jim said, "Let's head back now and wait for dark, okay?" The cover in their current location was solid, the bush densely shaded, but they'd be sitting ducks if they tried to get any closer in broad daylight. He said, "I don't want to risk this freak spotting us."

As he said it the guy came out of the barn, moving with the same body-proud swagger Jim had seen on gangbangers in the yard at Kingston pen. A couple of the Rottweilers started barking when they saw him, and the man strode up to the kennel gate and unhooked something from the latch post, a black club of some kind — a cattle prod, Jim realized — and now he raked it across the chain-link, creating a gout of sparks that silenced the dogs. He kicked dirt at them, then replaced the prod on its hook and went into the house.

Jim said, "Seen enough?"

But Dean was adamant. "I just want to take a closer look, then we're out of here."

Jim said, "Come on, man, this is close enough," and Dean said, "Fuck it," and charged into the field with the pistol aimed at the house. The Rottweilers were on their feet in an instant, barking in alarm.

Cursing, Jim backtracked a few meters into the bush to pick up a rusted length of rebar he'd spotted in the leaf litter on the way in, thinking if the shit hit the fan he could use it as a weapon.

* * *

Even as Dean moved he knew it was insane, rushing into the unknown like this, but all he could think about was killing this twisted son of a whore, making him pay for ending Trish's life. As he raced across the uneven ground, trying to hold his aim steady, he remembered their last conversation, Trish playfully describing their future together, him working in the ER and her in her veterinary practice, joking about which one of them was going to stay home with the babies and the seventeen cats they were going to own—

Dean felt something bump his chest.

Then he heard a loud report, a huge sound that cracked through the shallow valley and rolled back from the distant hills.

* * *

Jim saw it happen on his way back to the tree line with the rebar in his hand—Dean running hard, halfway to the farmhouse when the bullet ripped through his chest, the impact spinning him around bare milliseconds before the report reached Jim's ears—and Jim sank into a crouch on the forest floor, seeing Dean's eyes now, round with mortal surprise, seeming to search the tree line as he sagged to his knees, then fell face first into the tall grass, vanishing from Jim's line of sight.

Jim's initial impulse was to run to him, but a deeper instinct made him hesitate. To show himself out there now would be suicide—and truth be told, in that instant, with his daughter murdered and his best friend bleeding in the weeds, suicide by psychopath didn't seem like such a bad alternative.

Jim clutched his paltry weapon and stared at the spot where Dean had fallen, seeing no movement through the obscuring grass, feeling the gallop of his heart and the hot rush of air in his chest and realizing that in this moment the only thing he wished for more than his own death was a chance to kill the sick fuck who'd destroyed the people he loved.

He noticed movement to his right through the heat shimmer now, and shifted his gaze to the house.

The killer came down the steps into the sunlight, seeming to materialize out of the deep shadow of the porch, the ballcap and sunglasses gone now. He held a scope-equipped rifle in a trail carry and looked about thirty, all sinew and bone in a strappy T-shirt and faded jeans, gleaming eyes narrowed in a hunter's squint. He glanced at the charred remains of an old bench seat at the edge of the yard, then ambled toward Dean, those eyes constantly scanning.

Jim shrank deeper into the underbrush, fear leeching his rage. The man looked invincible, unperturbed at having just shot another human being, and Jim despised himself for being afraid. A still-sick part of him wanted to flee, back to the bottle and its promise of detachment. And who would be left to judge him if he did?

Then a tiny voice in his head, his own voice, saying, *Me*.

The man stopped at the patch of grass where Dean had fallen and pointed the rifle at him, then toed the body with his boot. Satisfied, he shifted the weapon into a sling carry and stooped to retrieve the .22. He tucked the pistol into his belt and stood, still tracking every compass point with those nimble eyes. He lingered a moment, rubbing the charms on a necklace Jim knew were made of human teeth, then started back toward the house, in no hurry.

But then he paused and Jim tensed, the man coming back now, skirting Dean to follow his tracks through the trampled weeds.

As quietly as he could, Jim crabbed his way deeper into the undergrowth, watching through a break in the foliage as the man paused at the tree line where Dean had crouched, sweeping his foot through the flattened grass and mumbling to himself, looking back at his property as if to duplicate the intruder's point of view, perhaps wondering what he might have seen.

He was just standing there now, seeming almost meditative, as if immersed in thought—*or perhaps just listening*—and Jim clutched the rebar, gauging his chances of rushing the man and beating him down before he could bring that rifle to bear. It was a ten-foot sprint through tangled underbrush, and he'd first have to get to his feet without being heard, no small task in these sun-parched brambles.

And right now even Jim's breathing sounded loud to him, huge and raspy and betraying, and he sucked in a stealthy lungful and held it, in that moment certain the man really *was* listening, his stillness almost preternatural, as if he'd somehow melded with the scene, slipped into some sort of sensory oneness with his surroundings and simply *knew* that Jim was out here somewhere.

As if to drive that perception home, the man moved deeper into the bush, his gaze keen and unblinking. At one point he passed within a foot of Jim's position and Jim realized he was still holding his breath, the urge to release it almost overmastering now.

Then the man angled away, doubling back toward the house, and Jim breathed and tried not to vomit.

* * *

Bobcat came back to the kid bleeding in the grass and bent to search him for ID or maybe a cell phone, anything to tell him if trouble was coming. But the kid had nothing on him, not even change in his pockets.

Fucker's just a boy, Bobcat thought, standing now, fascinated by the sheen of sunlight on the blood in the weeds. So what was he doing *here*, storming the house in broad daylight with his little bean shooter? Playing the hero?

Then it dawned and Bobcat said, "Boyfriend." He must've grabbed the kid's girl at some point and the little dipshit found out. But how? And how had he tracked him here?

Bobcat thought, *The trading post.* He'd just come from there. Could the kid have figured out what the carvings were made of and just hung around the place waiting for him to come back? *Fuck, no.* That was stupid. It didn't make sense.

So how had the kid put it together? Had he witnessed one of the snatches? Hitchhiking with those two little toads maybe, hiding in the trees till they got somebody to stop? Or just in there taking a piss? But no, he would've had plenty of time to come back out and grab a ride with them, and the toads wouldn't have left him behind.

What about that flag girl?

No. Wrong guy.

Rattled, Bobcat started back to the house, screaming at the Rotties to shut the fuck up, his mind whirling out of control now. He had to grab hold, think this thing through. Under the circumstances, *how* the kid had found him didn't matter as much as the fact that he'd been found. And if one asshole showed up, others would follow. It was just a matter of time.

His location was compromised. He had to move.

He went inside and leaned the rifle by the door, thinking he'd take the camper and leave the pickup behind, shoot those damned dogs, burn this place to the ground and head back to Louisiana, set up shop down there. He might have to do some other kind of work for a while, until he found an outlet for the carvings—although the Internet scheme Hank had come up with was working out pretty well—maybe poach gators like his daddy taught him when he was a kid.

Whatever it was, he could make it work.

It felt good to have a plan, his mind calming itself now, moving on to list the things he'd want to take with him, the chores that needed doing before he left.

But it was coming on to sundown now and he was hungry and he was tired. He'd dispose of the kid at first light—and maybe dig up the old hermit he'd 'borrowed' the farm from and burn him along with the house, let the cops find his bones and call it a mattress fire—then pack up the camper and hit the road. Sunday tomorrow. Twenty-four hours driving time, eight hours a day would put him back home in St. Francisville by Tuesday night, Wednesday morning at the latest.

Jesus Christ, Louisiana in July, hot as a motherfucker.

Sammy came into the kitchen now, toenails clicking on the linoleum, and Bobcat bent to scratch the little guy's neck, laughing as he always did when the mutt's tail sped up to double time, Bobcat saying, "What do you want for supper, little buddy? You want hot dogs? Boar's Head franks?" The terrier barked it's approval and Bobcat stood, saying, "Franks it is." He opened the fridge and brought out the weiners, earning another cheerful bark from the dog.

Getting a saucepan out of the cupboard, Bobcat said, "You're gonna like it down south, Sambo. You're gonna like it a lot."

* * *

Jim broke cover to watch the shooter return to the house. He waited until he heard the clap of the screen door, then crept back to the tree line, picturing his forehead in the crosshairs of that rifle scope now.

After mounting the steps, the man had seemed to vanish into the shadow of the porch, and Jim wondered if the slam of that door had merely been a ruse intended to draw him out. The man had shot Dean from that same pocket of shadow—Jim had seen the muzzle flash out of the corner of his eye as Dean fell—and at this very moment the killer might be getting ready to do the same thing to him. It was simple logic. If there *were* anyone else hiding out here, it would only be natural for that person to want to check on his fallen companion as quickly as possible. A shrewd hunter would do whatever it took to create a false sense of security in his intended victim—like slamming that screen door—and then *bam*. Lights out.

Still, the temptation to check on Dean was huge...but he decided to sit tight, at least for the time being.

Furious, frustrated, he sat with his back against a tree and stretched out his legs. His vantage here was perfect, affording him clear sightlines to both Dean's position and the farmhouse. And if Dean moved or if Jim even *thought* Dean moved, he'd belly-crawl the fifty yards out to him and let the chips fall where they may.

Last Call

Jim didn't wear a watch, but the sun was low in the west now and the shadows were growing longer. In an hour, maybe two, it'd be dark enough to—

To what?

Check on Dean, of course.

Coward.

Okay, yes, he was afraid. Terrified. Who wouldn't be? Waiting for that bullet to come.

But his every instinct told him Dean was dead. And if he ran out there now and got himself shot, what purpose would it serve? He couldn't avenge Dean and Trish if he was dead, too.

He got his cell phone out and flipped it open, common sense telling him that what he *should* be doing right now was calling the cops. But a deeper, colder part of him couldn't abide that idea. Besides, there was no signal on his cell, no surprise out here in the back country.

He tucked the phone away and picked up the rebar, liking its heft, his original plan—to wait until the killer fell asleep, then go in there and shoot him in the skull with the .22—playing out in his imagination, but with the rebar now instead of the gun. Go in there and drive a spike into that sick mind, eliminate even the remotest possibility that some canny defense lawyer might eventually squeeze the guy out through some unforeseeable loophole.

No, this piece of shit was going to pay for what he'd done. And Jim was going to collect the debt.

But the rebar wasn't going to do it.

He shifted his gaze to the outbuildings, thinking there was bound to be a nice heavy axe waiting in one of them. Or a pitch fork. Something with a little more reach than this stubby hunk of metal. He just had to wait for nightfall.

With a last look at the grass where Dean lay dead or dying, Jim got to his feet and faded back into the bush, angling through the trees toward the outbuildings now.

* * *

Bobcat ate a few hotdogs, then sat on the back porch to smoke a Cigarillo and watch the sun go down. But the franks weren't agreeing with him, sitting in his gut like a sauna stone now, and he didn't like the way the Rotties were looking at him, all of them pacing the fence, glaring at him like they knew what was coming. And maybe they did.

His old friend the bobcat made one of its rare appearances as the hills took the sun and the horizon began to bleed, the cat trotting through the yard bold as you please with a rabbit in its jaws, sparing Bobcat a brief yellow glance as it hustled off with its prize. He'd miss that beauty.

The bugs found him when the full moon rose, and Bobcat flicked his cigar butt over the railing and went inside to chug some Pepto-Bismol.

* * *

Last Call

In the thin creep of light from the farmhouse windows, Jim watched the killer toss his smoke into the night, the ember arcing out through space to land in the dooryard, spewing sparks as it bounced off the hard pack. Then he watched him go back inside, moving like a man who'd done a hard day's work and wanted only to rest.

Jim was still crouched at the tree line with the rebar in his hand, but closer to the outbuildings now, the barn only about twenty yards from his position. He'd seen the bobcat earlier, scooting into the barn with its dinner, and wondered if the animal had a litter hidden in there somewhere. The sleek cat had ducked under the camper before Jim lost sight of it, and every once in a while he thought he could hear the faint mewling of kittens, the sound eerily human, like the plaintive cries of a newborn.

The mosquitoes were swarming him now, and he decided it was time to move. A lone drift of cumulus had shrouded the moon, dimming its silvery light, and he knew there wasn't going to be a better time.

Jim rose to his full height, the muscles of his thighs punishing him for the bad posture, and started down the shallow incline to the barn, his movements quick and silent. His foot came down in standing water in a wheel rut, then he was in the shadow of the building as the moon shed its cover, burnishing the night again.

He slipped in through the open archway, losing sight of the house now, and in the moonlight saw an old Chevy pickup parked to the right of the camper. It made him wonder if the guy was sharing the house with someone; but once his eyes adjusted, he could just make out a set of heavy-duty snow tires on the Chevy and assumed the killer stored the camper for the winter and used the pickup instead.

Jim got moving again, squeezing along the narrow corridor between the barn wall and the campervan, feeling in the dark for an axe or a spade, anything he could use as a weapon. But there was nothing.

On the far side of the camper, he caught his toe on a hard edge and stumbled, losing his grip on the rebar as he flailed for balance. The rebar struck the barn floor with a hellish clatter, metal against metal, the sound carrying in the rural quiet, and Jim cursed under his breath, certain the blunder was going to cost him his life.

He froze, snatched a breath and listened—

And thought he heard a voice—*"Please"*—the sound distant and weak, seeming to emanate from beneath his feet.

Jim took out his cell phone and flipped it open, directing the dim glow of the screen at his shoes. He was standing on the edge of a large metal plate of the sort city workers used to cover excavations in the street, this one extending out of sight beneath the camper. Sinking to a crouch, he aimed the light under the vehicle and saw that a series of one-inch holes had been drilled through the plate, and he thought, *Air holes.*

He lay on his belly and shimmied partway under the camper, shining the light through one of the holes, whispering, "Is somebody down there?"

And Trish said, "Dad?"

Jim felt tears scorch his eyes. "Trish? Oh my God, is that you?"

"Yes, yes, Daddy, it's me...I knew you'd come."

He could hear her moving down there now, her feet shifting in water, but he couldn't see her, the light too dim.

He said, "Hang on, sweetheart, I'm going to get you out of there," and Trish said, "Dad, he's crazy," and Jim said, "I know." He said, "Sit tight, baby, I'm going to have to move this plate."

He wiggled out from under the vehicle and had a terrible moment when it occurred to him that one or more of the camper's wheels might be resting on the metal plate. But a quick inspection dispelled his worry and he thought, *Thank God.*

In the light of the cell phone he noticed an aluminum extension ladder propped against the wall, a hefty woodsplitting maul leaning next to it, and now he bent to his task, slipping his fingers under the edge of the plate and heaving with all of his strength. But the plate didn't budge, not even a fraction, and he cursed and tried to think.

There was a vertical support beam next to the camper and Jim sat with his back to it, wedging his heels against the edge of the plate and pushing with everything he had.

The plate shifted, moving about a foot and a half to reveal a narrow crescent of darkness, just enough room for Jim to stick his head in and shine the light down on his daughter. And what he saw filled him with rage, almost turning his stomach.

Trish was down there, wobbling on her feet, looking up at him with lidded eyes, every inch of her wasted frame caked in mud, her bare feet submerged in filthy water. She was naked and shivering and her cheeks were caved in, and even though he could see that she was too far down for him to reach, he extended his hand to her, reaching into the pit as far as he could; and when she raised her own hand Jim could see that she barely had the strength left to do it. But she did.

There was still five feet of space between their questing fingertips.

Jim said, "There's a ladder," and stood, saying, "I'll be right back," his heart breaking when he heard Trish say, "Please hurry, before he comes back."

He got the ladder and slid it in through the gap, telling Trish to be careful it didn't hit her on the head. When it was firmly planted in the pit, Jim shone the light down there and said, "Okay, Trish, come on up. Come on up, honey, and we'll get the hell out of here." She nodded and grasped the ladder rails, pulling her right foot out of the muck to rest on the bottom rung, her thin arms trembling as she tried to pull herself up. Jim said, "Come on, sweetheart. Dean's car is parked right down the road. Climb up out of there now and we're gone. We'll bring the cops down on this animal and they'll put him away for a dozen lifetimes."

But when she tried to get her left foot up, her right one skidded on the rung and she toppled into the water, the last of her strength spent.

Last Call

Jim said. "Okay, don't worry, kid. I'm coming down to get you."

But the space was too small, and he had to brace himself against the beam again and give the plate another shove, the effort gaining him only a few more inches, the far edge of the plate coming up hard against the barn wall.

But it was enough.

Jim backed into the yawning space until his foot found a rung. Then he was in the pit up to the hips, reaching for the next rung, seconds away from holding his daughter. There was a bad moment when it felt as if his trunk had gotten stuck between the plate and the rim of the pit, but he forced out his breath and squeezed through, bumping his head on the plate without feeling it, taking the rungs in precarious lunges—

Then he was lifting his child out of the muck, kissing the top of her head, holding onto her for dear life.

* * *

Yawning, Bobcat stacked the last of his belongings by the front door and thought, *To hell with it, I'll load up in the morning.*

But they were calling for rain through the night and he decided to get it over with now. He grabbed his Maglite off the workbench and glanced out the window, the moon illuminating the world out there like a muted spot, and he thought that one last walk in the cool country dark might be pleasant. Besides, the Maglite always stirred up the dogs, and if he set them off now he wouldn't get a wink of sleep.

He left the flashlight on the bench and went outside to get the camper.

* * *

Jim said, "Okay, Trish, it's time to go." It stunk down here, feces floating in the foul water, and Jim couldn't imagine how she'd managed to survive in these conditions. A healthy person could go a few weeks without food, but without water...

He pictured his daughter forced to drink the slop they were standing in and wanted to drown that bastard in it.

Trish was shivering, falling asleep standing up, and Jim took off his shirt and put it on her, buttoning it up to her neck, its curved tail long enough to cover her bottom. It wasn't much but it would have to do.

He bent to lift her into his arms—and heard footfalls scuffing into the barn.

Jim pressed his hand over Trish's mouth and froze.

The killer was directly above them now, moving along that narrow corridor on the driver's side of the camper—the metal plate rocking under his weight, grit sifting down into their upturned faces—and when Trish uttered a fearful moan Jim pressed his lips to her ear and whispered, "Please be quiet, baby, please be quiet..."

Then the guy opened the van door and climbed inside, pulling the door shut with a slam that startled Jim so badly he almost cried out.

Now the engine turned over and the headlights came on, smoky cones of light angling down through the air holes on the reek of exhaust, and Jim played out the next few seconds in his mind, seeing the killer turn his head to back the van out of the barn—or using the side mirrors to get it done—praying he wouldn't glance back into the barn; because if he did, he'd see that the plate had been moved and he'd get out of the camper and kill them both, shoot them like rats in a rain barrel.

Jim held his breath and stared at the metal plate. He heard the clunk of the shifter as it dropped into gear, then the clangor of the front tires coming onto the plate—in his mind's eye he saw the right front wheel plunging into the gap he'd created up there—but the plate held and the camper cleared the mouth of the pit.

Jim breathed, whispering to Trish, "Almost over now, honey. Almost over…"

The grumble of the engine receded, the glare of the headlights intensifying briefly, then fading to darkness as the vehicle pulled away from the barn.

Jim picked Trish up, slung her arms around his neck and told her to hang on tight. Then he stepped onto the ladder and climbed to the top, using one arm to support her legs and the other to clutch the rail, appalled at how little she weighed.

At the top he had to brace himself to push Trish out through the opening, and now she lay out there at the edge of the pit, too exhausted to move. Jim said, "Trish, I need you to move so I can get out," and after a moment she did, rolling away from the hole.

Then Jim was out too, bearing her up, heading for the barn door, the woods, the car and freedom.

Limp in his arms, Trish said, "Where's Dean?" and Jim paused at the tree line, knowing he'd have to tell her but not wanting to do it now. What he wanted right now was to get her as far away from here as he could. Get her to safety. That was all that mattered.

But he said, "Sweetheart, Dean is dead. The bastard shot him."

Trish stiffened in his arms, lifting her head off his shoulder now to lock eyes with him in the moonlight. She said, "Where is he, Dad? We can't let that monster have him. Are you sure he's dead?"

An old voice in his head: *Say yes.*

"I'm almost certain. The bastard shot him, honey, right through the chest. Dean went running into the yard with a gun in his hand and the guy shot him. I could see where he fell but I couldn't get to him. I watched for a long time but he didn't move. Trish, we should—"

She said, "Dad, put me down. Put me down and show me where he is."

"Trish—"

"I'm not leaving without him."

Jim thought, *Shit*, but he knew she was right. He wanted to tell her they could call for help from the road—and if push came to shove, he could easily carry her out of here against her will and pray she didn't hold it against him later on—but he knew she'd never forgive him. And in thinking it, knew that he'd never forgive himself. If there was even an outside chance that Dean was still alive, he owed it to the kid to find out. Even if it cost him his life.

He set Trish on her feet. "Alright, listen. I'm going to run back there and get him. Dead or alive, I won't leave him here, I promise."

"Okay."

He gave her the keys to the Beemer and pointed into the woods. "The road is straight back that way. Dean's car is out there. If I'm not back in twenty minutes—" he dug the phone out of his pocket and handed it to her, flipping it open so she could see the time "—I want you to *promise* me you'll go find the car and get the hell out of here, dial nine-one-one as soon as you get a signal. But whatever you do, just drive, get as far away from here as you can, okay?"

Trish was looking down at the phone, nodding her head.

Jim lifted her chin, finding her eyes. "Trish, I need you to promise me."

She said, "I promise."

Jim looked toward the house, then back at Trish. "Alright. In the meantime I want you to stay out of sight. And no matter what you might hear or what you might see, you do *not* go anywhere near that place. Understood?"

Trish nodded again.

"Okay. I'll be right back."

"Dad?"

"Yes, honey?"

She hugged him with feeble strength, then pressed something into his hand. A jackknife. He hadn't even realized she was holding it.

She said, "It's his. I stole it from him."

Jim thanked her and slipped the knife into his pocket, already planning to arm himself with something a good deal heftier than a jackknife.

He kissed Trish on the forehead, then led her into the bush and eased her down onto a drift of leaves. He said, "Rest here awhile, okay? And keep an eye on the time."

As he started away, Trish said, "Be careful, Dad. He's an animal."

Jim said, "I will," and went back to the barn for the splitting maul.

* * *

He doubled back through the woods with the axe in his hand, the going slow even with the moon hanging straight overhead now, and it occurred to him as he picked his way through the underbrush that twenty minutes might have been an optimistic limit to impose on himself. But above everything else, he wanted Trish out of here, and he knew that if Dean were still alive he'd want the same thing.

When he got back to Dean's take off point, Jim hunkered down and spent another few minutes watching the farmhouse for any signs of movement; but everything looked quiet down there now, most of the interior lights extinguished. Even the Rottweilers were peaceful, sleeping under the moon.

It was now or never.

Moving in a crouch, Jim followed Dean's trail through the tall grass. A rodent of some kind, a field mouse or a vole, skittered across his path, and Jim's skin crawled in cold handfuls, his nerve's drawn wire tight.

And just when it seemed he'd never find Dean, there he was, face down in the moonlight and deathly still; and when Jim touched his skin it was cold, so cold that it startled him and he recoiled into the weeds, scraping his elbow on the blade of the maul.

Resuming his crouch, Jim tried to compose himself, Trish's voice in his head now, telling him to check for a pulse, and he did, pressing two fingers into the hollow of the kid's neck, feeling only that cadaverous cold—

Then something twitched against his fingertips, faint and faraway, and Jim wondered if he'd imagined it. But there it was again.

A pulse.

Jim was no doctor, but he guessed it couldn't have been much more than thirty beats a minute, dreadfully weak in a blood vessel that should have been bounding with life. He'd read about hypothermia somewhere, people surviving exposure by lapsing into a state akin to hibernation, the temperature drop protecting the brain.

Excitement flared in Jim's gut, eclipsing a wave of shame, and he rolled Dean onto his back, the kid limp and covered in blood, the stuff clotted now, glimmering like obsidian in the moonlight. Facing the farmhouse, he hoisted Dean into a fireman's carry and bent to retrieve the maul—

A brilliant point of light detonated like a supernova, bathing the yard in a seething glare, and now a harsh voice said, "Drop the kid. The axe, too. Hands where I can see 'em."

Shading his eyes, Jim saw the killer step off the porch like a dark angel, the rifle aimed at the ground. He let go of the maul, lay Dean in the wild grass and put his hands on his head, the source of that light resolving into focus as his eyes adjusted, a cluster of Klieg carbon arc lamps perched high atop a power pole behind the kennel, the same kind of floods they used in the yard in Kingston. Facing death, Jim wondered absently why he hadn't noticed them before now.

The dogs were up and howling and now the killer was waving Jim closer, beckoning him into the bald patch of dooryard. Resigned, Jim did as he was told, moving deeper into that stark dome of light, a glaring oasis in the trench of the night.

Now the guy said, "That's far enough," and Jim stopped six feet away from him, close enough to spit in that smug face. The man was a full head taller than him, with long bandy limbs and huge hands. He lowered the rifle and said, "Who was the bitch to you?"

"My daughter."

He gave a little nod. "How'd you find me?"

"The carvings. The cops found one in her car."

"Oh, *that* little bitchcat." Grinning now, showing perfect white teeth. "Wasn't she the feisty one?"

"Sick fuck."

The guy said, "Call me Bobcat," and rubbed his jaw, as if considering the problem at hand. Then he raised the rifle to a firing position and peered into the scope, the single dark eye of the bore only three feet from Jim's face now, aimed at the space between his eyes.

Bobcat said, "Well, I guess I'd like to stand out here all night and chinwag with you, Dad, but see, you're trespassing, and I shoot trespassers."

He cocked the rifle and Jim closed his eyes, waiting for the bullet, his last thought reserved for his daughter and the gratitude he felt in knowing she'd survive.

Then he heard the man scuffing through the dirt, and opened his eyes to see him lean the rifle against the kennel fence. One of the dogs threw itself at the chain-link, snarling at him, and Bobcat cursed the animal and kicked dust in its face, backing it off. Then he returned his attention to Jim.

Jim dropped his hands to his sides, curling them into fists.

Bobcat said, "But in your case, seeing as you're family, I'm going to fuck you up the old fashioned way." He moved to the center of the yard, spreading his arms as if in supplication. "Gonna beat you to death. Bare knuckle. How'd that be?"

Jim said, "Works for me," and waded in.

Lightning quick, Bobcat went for the sucker punch and Jim blocked it and got inside, jabbing the man's eye and driving an elbow up as he stepped away, cracking Bobcat on the nose and drawing blood. Bobcat staggered back, cuffing blood off his lips in mild surprise. He opened his mouth to say something and Jim kicked him in the chest with the flat of his foot, knocking him on his ass in the dirt.

Jim glanced at the rifle against the fence and Bobcat was on his feet, standing between Jim and the gun now, grinning through bright red blood. He said, "You're pretty good," and spat at Jim's feet.

Jim thought, *That's it, asshole. Get mad.* The fucker was hard as nails and had a good six inches of reach on him; but he was cocky, and every man Jim had ever beaten in a street fight had been cocky.

Bobcat feinted with a lunge and threw a kick at Jim's groin. Jim caught his foot and continued its skyward momentum, felling him onto his back again, harder this time, knocking the wind out of him.

Squinting up at Jim, jets of night-vapor on his breath as he fought for air, Bobcat said, "I'm gonna hurt you for that. I'm really gonna hurt you for that."

"Better get off your ass, then."

Bobcat got up and shot a bloody snot rocket through his nostril, that antic light gone from his eyes now, replaced by flint and deadly intent. In the kennel the dogs were losing their minds, snarling and trying to gnaw through the chain-link.

He came straight at Jim with his fists up and Jim missed his bobbing head with a couple of jabs. Bobcat tagged him with a stinging kick to the inner thigh, then clamped that big left hand around his throat and drove him backward into the chain-link, closing off his air. Jim grabbed the man's wrist, but it was like grabbing an iron bar and Bobcat slapped him on the ear with an open hand, setting off a high-pitched whine in his skull. Jim tried to kick him and Bobcat pulled Jim's face into a rising knee, then flung him rag-like to the ground.

Jim was stunned but up fast, throwing a couple of wild jabs that connected with nothing. Bobcat shoved him away, accelerating his trajectory with a kick to the midsection, slamming him into the fence again. Jim sank to his knees, the world spinning now, and felt something under his shin in the weeds fringing the kennel. Bobcat rushed in hard and Jim came up with an old stainless steel dog bowl in his hands, driving its stout rim into Bobcat's throat, backing him off long enough to gain his feet and grab the rifle. He dropped the bowl to bring the gun around and Bobcat kicked it out his hands.

Jim said, *"Fuck,"* and Bobcat struck him with a powerful left. Badly hurt now, Jim wobbled and saw stars, his legs wanting to fail him. To this point he'd been trying to corral his rage, mete out punishment with clarity and precision; but he was tiring now and his opponent seemed unfazed by the beating he'd taken so far, and Jim could contain his fury no longer, could actually *see* it bleeding into his vision in a crimson tide.

He put his head down and plowed like a ram into the man's midsection, feeling the top of his head hit a plank hard abdomen, and now those long arms closed around his middle and lifted him off the ground. Then he was down on his back with Bobcat straddling him, Bobcat raining blow after blow into his face, Jim barely able to raise his arms to protect himself.

With a howl of frustration Jim bucked under Bobcat's weight, got his hands up around the man's neck and pulled his face down close to his own, his teeth finding a knob of chin in that scruff of beard, seizing on it with the full force of his fury. Bobcat squealed and stopped swinging, trying to pull away now, and Jim savored the hot rush of blood that filled his mouth and heard his own roar eclipse the clamor of the dogs. Bobcat rolled onto his back, taking Jim with him, breaking his grip and frog-kicking him in the chest, Jim coming to his feet as he back-pedalled away.

Barely able to stand now, Jim spat a chunk of hairy meat into the dirt and watched Bobcat roll toward the kennel, thinking he was going to release the dogs. Then he had the rifle in his hands and he looked like some terrible, blood-drenched Reaper, staggering closer to deliver Jim's death.

Instead, he swung the rifle by the barrel, the heavy oak butt striking Jim in the temple, dropping him to the ground. He squinted at Bobcat coming out of the glare of the Kliegs and knew that he'd done all he could and had lost.

But Bobcat wasn't through with him yet.

"What'd you think," he said, circling Jim now, the rifle aimed at the ground. "You could *beat* me? Waltzing into my shit like you belong here." He stomped on Jim's chest and Jim felt something snap in there. "Biting like a little girl. Well, you're here now, Pop. How do you like it?" He kicked Jim in the head and Jim felt himself going. "Huh? How do you like it?"

The Rottweilers were yowling and slavering in the harsh light and Bobcat turned to them and said, "You want this piece of meat? Don't want me to—" kicking Jim again "—tenderize it a bit more for you first?"

Exhausted, barely conscious now, Jim saw the man grasp his own teeth and try to wiggle them. Heard him say, "Huh, Krazy Glue. Amazing shit."

Then Bobcat grabbed him by the ankle and started dragging him toward the kennel, Bobcat saying, "Play fight's over."

The light was scorching Jim's eyes, filling them with tears, and he felt a crushing weight of regret for Dean, a young man he'd come to love and whose death was now on his head. Broken, defeated, he gazed at Bobcat through wet prisms, the warrior triumphant, and saw one of the dogs snap at him through the narrow space between the gate and the latch post. He saw the man remove the cattle prod from its hook and jab it into the dog's muzzle, watched the animal yelp and slink away.

Bobcat's back was to him now and Jim remembered the jackknife. With the final shreds of his will, he reached into his pocket and brought it out, almost dropping it in the dirt. He opened the blade and concealed it with his wrist, waiting for his chance.

Bobcat unlatched the gate and turned his head to face Jim. In the same instant Jim sat up and drove the blade into the back of the man's knee. Bobcat shrieked, losing his grip on Jim's ankle, and now he jabbed the prod into the side of Jim's head, the jolt disconnecting his brain, slamming him nerveless and quivering into the dirt, his connection to this bedlam in the night all but shattered now, more dreamlike than real.

Bobcat cursed and grabbed the gate to slam it shut. As the halves of the latch touched, the stung Rottweiler head-butted the gate open and sank its teeth into Bobcat's calf. Bobcat screamed and swung the prod, missing his mark as the dog jerked with its powerful jaws, tipping him sideways into the dirt and dragging him partway into the kennel, the other dogs closing in now.

Jim tried to move, tried to lift his leg to kick the gate shut, but he had nothing left.

Clutching the latch post with his free hand, Bobcat rolled onto his back as a second dog seized his other leg, the combined power of the infuriated animals breaking his grip on the post and dragging him deeper into the kennel, forcing his legs apart like a wishbone. A third dog came for his crotch and Bobcat zapped it with the prod, then went after the others, jolting them one by one and screaming them down, crabbing his way back toward the gate as the dogs relented. Then he scrambled to his feet and turned to face the gate.

Trish was there now, a tarnished ghost in a man's shirt, and she slammed the gate shut, ran the padlock through the latch holes and locked it down with a *snap*. Then she picked up the rifle and aimed it at Bobcat's face.

What followed was an instant of freeze-frame, in real time no longer than a heartbeat and yet eerily spun out, animal and human intimately entwined in a static tableau: Bobcat realizing he was caught; Trish with her finger on the trigger, deciding; the dogs yielding to the conditioned outcome of conflict with their master while Jim lay beaten on the ground.

It was one of the Rottweilers that broke the spell, the big male with the star-shaped marking on its chest. Swaying, a fierce growl issuing from deep in its throat, it stood at the apex of a ragged V of dogs and turned its head, first left, then right, as if seeking assent from its kennel mates. Then it lunged, its vice-like jaws clamping around Bobcat's wrist, the cattle prod clattering to the ground at his feet. Bobcat screamed—Jim could actually hear the bones in the man's wrist splintering like tinder—and bent to retrieve the prod.

Then the dogs were on him, bearing him down as they had Julie, ripping flesh from bone. Hopelessly pinned, Bobcat thrust out a beseeching hand, screaming, "Shoot the dogs, *shoot the fucking dogs*," and Trish said, "Asshole," and dropped the rifle in the dirt.

Bobcat was still screaming when Trish came over to Jim and did her best to help him to his feet. When he was up Jim hugged her tight, scolding her gently for coming down here, then kissed her and thanked her for saving his life.

After a moment they hobbled over to Dean. In the glare of the Kliegs Jim could see that the bullet had shattered the kid's clavicle, then exited high on his shoulder.

Jim used his undershirt to fashion a crude pressure dressing, knotting the sleeves over the entry wound, and Dean moaned when he snugged it down tight.

A few feet away Trish stood spellbound, watching the dogs maul her kidnapper, and now Jim rose to block her view and hold her close.

Then, calling on a final reserve of strength, he picked Dean up and carried him into the farmhouse, telling Trish to wait in the kitchen. He lugged Dean down the hallway to a big room at the front of the house, seeing the barber chair now and the workbench and the little dog drowsing in its basket. He lay Dean on a threadbare couch, covered him with a blanket and told him he was going to get help, hoping the kid could hear him. He found an old rotary phone in the kitchen and used it to dial 911. The dispatcher seemed to know the area and Jim told her to hurry, his friend had been shot and his daughter was in shock.

He found another blanket and wrapped it around Trish's shoulders. She told him she wanted to wait with Dean and Jim brought her to him, lifting the kid's head off the couch so she could sit with it in her lap. Then he went back to the kitchen to get her some water.

Filling a glass from the tap, Jim glanced at the kennel through the window over the sink, Bobcat silent out there now, the dogs rag-dolling his savaged remains.

Then he brought the water to Trish and pulled up a chair to wait with her.

* * *

A short while later, an orange and white air ambulance settled in the floodlit backyard, the downwash from the rotors raising eddies of litter and dust. Jim led the paramedics to Dean, who was semiconscious now and in a great deal of pain. They took his vitals, attached him to oxygen and IV fluids and bundled him onto a stretcher. They told Trish they'd be right back with a stretcher for her, but she insisted on walking. Jim helped her along. At the ambulance doors Trish asked him if he was coming to the hospital with them and Jim said he should probably wait for the cops to show up. "I'll see you there later," he said.

As the chopper lifted off, Jim went back into the house to call Sally. She picked up on the first ring, her voice shrill and expectant.

"Yes?"

Jim's voice broke when he said, "Sal, we found her. She's alive…"

* * *

Once the stretchers had been secured in the air ambulance, one of the paramedics went to work on Dean while another started an IV on Trish, the man saying, "You'll feel a needle pick now." But Trish felt nothing, just the smooth rubber gloves on his hands and an overwhelming sense of relief at being out of that stinking grave and away from the madman.

The paramedic cranked the IV open wide and Trish could feel the cool fluid flowing up her arm. There was chatter in the cockpit now, someone talking on the radio, the details muddied by the chop of the rotors...but Trish got the gist of it, a doctor on the other end giving instructions, telling the paramedics to apply pressure dressings to Dean's wounds and administer morphine for the pain, telling them to push fluids and use vasopressors as required.

When the initial commotion tapered off, the chopper moving at speed now, Trish reached across the space between the stretchers and found Dean's hand, ice cold and flaccid under a heating blanket, and gave it a gentle squeeze. At first there was no response, Dean lying stock still with his eyes closed, the fine mist from the oxygen they were giving him condensing on the whiskers around his mouth; but then she felt a feeble twitch, Dean's fingers flexing, and thought she heard him say her name, barely above a whisper.

She said, "Dean?"

"Trish..." he said again, she was sure of it now. "Will you marry me?"

Trish felt something inside of her spill out warm. But before she could respond, Dean's hand went slack and a paramedic said, "We've got an arrest," and now a curtain was drawn, blocking her view, and the commotion resumed in earnest.

* * *

After talking to Sally, Jim went outside to the front porch and sat on the steps, unwilling to spend another moment alone in the lunatic's lair. It was a beautiful night made eerie by the glow of the Klieg lamps, dimmer by half out here at the front of the house, edging the night mist in tattered, rainbow-hued halos. The camper was parked in the turnaround, and for a moment Jim wondered what might be hidden inside.

He was falling asleep on the steps when a black-and-white roared into the yard followed by a green sedan, and Jim stood, as worn out as he'd ever been. Two uniformed officers emerged from the cruiser, and Detective Boland got out of the sedan. The officers fanned out with their weapons drawn, the younger of the two making a beeline for the camper, the other looping around to the outbuildings. Boland came over to Jim.

"Jesus Christ, Jim," the detective said. "You look like you've been to war."

Jim said nothing.

Boland said, "Where is he?"

"Out back."

"Dead or alive?"

Jim just stared at him, dazed and exhausted, and Boland waved the young officer over. Weapons raised, the two men moved to the back of the house.

After a moment Jim followed. He paused at the edge of the back porch to watch the officer vomit in the dirt, Boland leaving the man to it, some primitive instinct compelling him to witness up close the blood frenzy in the kennel, the massive dogs tireless in the annihilation of their tormentor.

Turning his attention to the dogs, Jim wondered if they'd have to be put down, thinking they'd at least have to be sedated before anyone could get near what was left of Bobcat.

He stood there for what felt like a long time, drifting in and out, then Boland glanced at him with a kind of stoic approval and Jim hobbled over to join him. The men stood together in the weeds at the edge of the kennel and watched the dogs with unblinking eyes, most of the brutes tiring now, spent from their feral exertions, only the big male continuing the onslaught with any enthusiasm, working on Bobcat's neck now, attached to his unsprung torso by a twisted column of vertebrae and a few glistening tendons.

After a moment, Boland put his hand on Jim's shoulder and said, "All right, chum, let's get you to the hospital." Then he started away.

Before following, Jim took one last look at the killing floor and saw a silvery glint in the gape of Bobcat's mouth, Klieg light gleaming through Trish's tiny tooth diamond.

EPILOGUE

ON A MILD Sunday evening in May, Trish West sat in a circle of somber women in the basement of Sacred Heart Church, a ten-minute walk from the university. She'd regained most of the weight she'd lost down in the pit, and had a full set of perfect white teeth. She knew she looked healthy—she could see it in any mirror—but the youthful sparkle was gone from her eyes; replacing it was a grim watchfulness, a game animal's wariness. She could see that, too.

Tonight was her first visit to the group, but it was clear that everyone here knew who she was, many of them calling her by name as she mingled in the minutes before the meeting began. It was strange, an ordeal like hers ending in celebrity. 'The only girl to survive an encounter with *The Dentist*,' a moniker some reporter had given him that stuck. Her dad had suggested the group, and Trish agreed that it might be worth a try. For the first twenty minutes she listened to some pretty horrific stories—violent spouses, animal attacks, mutilating accidents—but by the time her turn came around, she knew she was in the right place.

She sat up straight in her chair and said, "Hi, everyone, my name is Trish and I'm a survivor."

The group said, "Hi, Trish."

She said, "It's been almost a year since the dogs took the monster's life. Watching him die, torn apart like that, was easy; in a sick way, even gratifying. I know he's gone, but getting him out of my head is another matter. Talking about it helps—that's why I'm here—but he's always with me. At night I close my eyes and I see him skinning that woman alive...

"When the story came out people were great, kind words and offers of support coming in from all over the world. The university's covering my tuition for the next three years and my dentist put in a full set of implants free of charge. Several good people offered to adopt the Rottweilers, but they were too far gone and had to be put down. I kept the Jack Russell for a while, but having him around was just too difficult. He's living with a nice old lady in Toronto now. Overall, I've been doing okay. My studies are going well and I'm starting to sleep again.

"But there's a twisted side to all of it, too. His carvings are selling on the Internet for thousands of dollars apiece now, and ghouls from Hollywood still track me down, offering quick fortunes for the movie rights to my story. But I only want it behind me. I lost myself. I almost lost my boyfriend." She gave a wan smile and held up her left hand, showing a small engagement diamond. "My fiancée now.

"But I found my father, and that's all I ever really wanted."

ABOUT THE AUTHOR

Sean Costello is the author of eight novels and numerous screenplays. His thriller *Here After* has been optioned to film by David Hackl, director of *Saw V*. Sean's horror novels have drawn comparisons to the works of Stephen King, and his thrillers to those of Elmore Leonard. In the real world he's an anesthesiologist, but if asked, he'd tell you he'd much rather be writing. All eight of his titles are currently available as ebooks, wherever ebooks are sold. Sean is currently hard at work on several new writing projects.

To stay up to date on the author's latest projects, sign up for his newsletter at www.seancostello.net.

Made in the USA
Middletown, DE
21 April 2016